Elmo

By Matt Shea

"Elmo," by Matt Shea. ISBN 978-1-62137-352-0 (Softcover); ISBN 978-1-62137-353-7 (Ebook).

Library of Congress Number on file with publisher.

Published 2013 by Virtualbookworm.com Publishing Inc., P.O. Box 9949, College Station, TX 77842, US.

Manufactured in the United States of America.

Dedication

THESE WRITINGS ARE DEDICATED to Kathleen Marie Shea.

"Kathy" is my big sister and definitely lives up to the billing. She is the 'queen bee' that watches over her five younger siblings while she provides a home for our parents and nurses them. She loves me with an unconditional love that pushes me to develop in all my endeavors. My sister watches me develop as a writer and offers encouragement. This puts wind in my sails as I do my best to illustrate how I feel this world can and should be.

Kathy applies such humanity to the *real world* which in turn inspired me to write this novel. My story is about a small town pulling together to survive, with youth joining the cause. Kathy Shea has been a nurse for over forty years and dedicates her free time to help others. Countries as far away as Hades, Vietnam, Honduras and Rwanda have been graced with her medical expertise and classic bed-side manner. Her wonderful husband, Johann Wassermann even travels with her when time allows.

In honor of how my sister, Kathy devotes her life to go as far and wide as possible to help others:

I hereby dedicate "Elmo" to Kathleen Marie Shea.

Kathy, I am grateful to know you and to especially have you as that big sister that watches over me. I love you with all my heart and hope that this book makes *you* feel good inside.

Tell Johann I say, "Hello!"

Love,
Mathew.

Contents

Chapter I 1

Chapter II 11

Chapter III... 16

Chapter IV 25

Chapter V 41

Chapter VI... 51

Chapter VII 62

Chapter VIII 74

Chapter IX 84

Chapter X.. 94

Chapter XI 101

Chapter XII 112

Chapter XIII.. 121

Chapter XIV.. 128

Chapter XV 137

Chapter XVI.. 141

Epilogue 151

Author Biography 152

Chapter 1

BEN SKATES LOOKED DOWN at the dinner table. The married man with two children did his very best to exemplify all was secure. Little did they know that their father had a secret life. *He* was the new panhandler that loitered at the corner of First and Elm Street; the one the teenagers called *Elmo*.

Elmo only came out at night and his identity was unknown. He became whoever was on shift to wear the hobo outfit and *beg* for any handout. The tattered costume was convincing from the oily black trench coat to the patched baggy pants with dull brown shoes. A large brimmed hat from the 1940s tilted forward over the ski mask that hid his shame. Shiny dark leather gloves further insulated the disguised panhandler from the winter chill.

The dads from Miner were all in on it. The ones that were fortunate enough to have work donated what they could to a community pot and still took shifts wearing the outfit. In their eyes, *all* were working hard to allow their families to survive.

Ben took his soft brown eyes off the meal and looked at his family. The heavy set man with graying hair and a bushy beard gave a warm smile. His high school sweetheart, Gloria, sat facing him. Her flowing brown hair and matching eyes still held the former Homecoming Queen's beauty. She was a supportive wife and was aware of the cutbacks on Ben's job. Gloria rose to the occasion by running a tight ship at home and saving spare change. What she didn't know was that months ago things got worse, forcing her husband to take odd jobs and panhandle at night.

To Ben's right was his 15-year-old daughter, Susan. She was definitely her mother's daughter possessing her beauty and charm. The teen's brown hair and matching eyes accented a lean pretty face with distinction. Susan was already a popular cheerleader and on the honor roll. Many believed she was destined to become a model.

To Ben's left was his son, Sam. The boy was months away from graduation with an enviable future. He was an exceptional pitcher and was a candidate for a scholarship to play college ball—a dream he'd held onto since childhood. However, there was more to the 17-year-old than baseball. He was also an honor student and blessed with the family genes. Like his father, Sam stood tall at six feet three inches. An athletic body graced the family's brown hair and eyes. He was sought after by every girl in the valley.

It was now time to say grace. Ben's mighty hands extended towards his children and they followed suit. A tight circle was formed with the four bowing down.

The head of household spoke. "Dear Lord, we are grateful for this meal and for this family. We are aware that you provide for us even through the darkest times. As you know, many are struggling to survive. Please continue to watch over everyone and guide us. Bless this meal and thank you."

"Amen," responded the table. The family released hands and sat up looking at one another with gratitude.

There was a brief moment of silence then Sam electrified the room. "Let's dig in!" he exclaimed.

The meatloaf with zesty barbeque sauce was a family favorite. It was accompanied with mashed potatoes smothered in brown gravy, green beans, buttered rolls, and a tossed salad to balance out the meal. As always, a pitcher of milk added the final touch. A free-for-all immediately took place at the festive dining table and once plates were filled, Gloria slowed down the tempo by addressing the children.

"How was school today?" asked the loving mother. Susan began to give a full account on what her day consisted of.

Sam eventually followed. He gave a brief update on how his classes were going and then he talked about his progress in baseball. The father had a gleam in his eye as he was listening because the Skates' name was locally famous for baseball. Ben himself set high school records years ago that broke his father's old marks. Sam easily broke his stats and was on track to surpass the former semi-pro star's career. Ben was proud.

Ben savored the moment as he sat back and watched his family. It was another winter evening at home with everyone present. More important, they were warm, happy, and being fed—a blessing that was being threatened.

Dinner continued with extra helpings passed around and more stories being told.

Soon the table was cleared and Gloria's homemade berry pie was served with vanilla ice cream off to the side.

"Thanks, mom!" cried out the brother and sister.

"Gloria, thank you for what you do for us," said the husband. "Nobody knows their way around a kitchen like you do."

Eventually dinner was over. It was six o'clock and Gloria went into the family room to watch her favorite television show. Sam and Susan did their after dinner chores: clearing the table and washing the dishes. When the last utensil was put away, Sam called out from the kitchen. "Dad, I am finished with my homework. Can I go out with my friends for a while?"

"I don't see why not," answered Ben. "Just remember that you have school tomorrow."

"Okay, dad," said the son. "Thanks!"

Susan called out next. "Mom, I am almost done with my homework. Can I have a friend over later?"

"Sure you can," said Gloria.

"Thanks, mom!" cried out the daughter.

The household was now spread out, with each member having separate plans.

Ben sat alone at the dining room table. This gave him more time to reflect on his problems and count his blessings. He was still, however, grateful for many things: they were all healthy, still had a home, and weren't going hungry—yet.

And thank God for Troy, Ben quietly thought to himself. *He still refuses to avoid me when I approach him."*

Troy Meeker was a friend of Ben's who served twenty five years in the Army and promptly retired. The lean man with short, curly red hair stood just over six feet tall. His black framed glasses personified an intellect from the 1950s and his sincere blue eyes displayed a compassion that showed he was available to everyone. The good man never married. Instead, he lived with his aging mother and looked after her. This dedication allowed him to understand the struggles that other families were going through. Troy eventually became a deacon in their church so as to serve God and the community in anyway fit.

Ben patted the pen pocket of his red flannel shirt that held two folded twenty dollar bills. His thought continued. *He must have lost track on how much I have borrowed from him; bless his soul...*

The tranquil moment was interrupted by a light tapping on the front door. Looking at the clock he realized that the recognizable sound could only be one person: Sharon Wilson. She was the sweet old lady that always baked cookies for the entire neighborhood. The widow that lived two doors down from him and always knew where to go when she needed help without losing her dignity. Sharon traditionally asked for five dollars; Ben always gave twenty.

The father got up from the table and walked to the living room. Approaching the entryway, he paused to gather his composure. With game face on, he opened the door. There before him stood Mrs. Wilson.

The petite woman barely stood over five feet tall with a forward lean to her stance. She wore a pink knitted ski hat that only allowed her Nordic-weathered face to be exposed. Matching pink gloves held a small black purse with a vintage gray wool coat keeping the old woman warm. Bright blue eyes peered through the intense cold as she looked up to her hero with hope. It was apparent that she was looking for a 'port in the storm.'

Ben looked at the woman he took grocery shopping once a week and could sense fear. The 72-year-old had no one and heavily relied on the man with broad shoulders.

The gentle giant immediately gave his patented ear to ear smile. "Good evening, Mrs. Wilson!" exclaimed Ben. "It's so good to see you. Would you please come in and get warm with us?"

The old woman was delighted with the reception. "Oh, I would love that," she said with a tone of relief. Her mood quickly changed as she leaned closer to him. "Ben," she cautiously spoke in a soft tone. "I am almost out of cat food and I will get my social security check the first of next month." Nervously she continued, "Five dollars would..."

Ben interrupted. "Mrs. Wilson, after all that you have done for us," he said with conviction. "The cookies you bake for us and the wonderful visits we get mean everything to us. Please accept this and do not worry about paying it back." The struggling father reached into his pen pocket and pulled out a folded twenty dollar bill. He handed it to her as she placed both hands over his. With direct eye contact, she thanked him for being so kind. She opened her tiny black purse and put the money inside.

"Now please come in and visit for a while," said Ben as he opened the door further. Happily, Sharon Wilson entered the home that always welcomed her.

"Let me help you get that coat of yours off," offered Ben. "Well hang it on the coat rack and let it get nice and warm."

Sharon took off her hat and gloves and placed them in her purse. Next she started to unbutton her coat as Ben stood behind to assist. In one motion he gracefully pulled off the opened garment and hung it on the rack.

By this time the rest of the family entered the living room to greet their guest.

"Hello, Mrs. Wilson," said Gloria. "What a wonderful surprise this is! Would you like to have some tea with us?"

The face of the lonely woman on a fixed income lit up. *This* was the only family she had. "Why, I'd love that!" she exclaimed.

"Hello, Mrs. Wilson," greeted a cheerful Sam.

"Hi, Mrs. Wilson," said Susan.

"Well hello everybody!" replied Sharon.

Ben walked towards the coffee table in the living room and pointed at a rocking chair closest to the fireplace. "Why don't you sit here and I'll get a fire going," suggested Ben.

"I'll make a pot of tea," said Gloria.

The old woman did find her port in the storm. She sat down in the rocker she always sat in and placed her purse on her lap. Tonight, Sharon Wilson would not be lonely; she would have an evening in front of a fireplace with loved ones. "I'll get some wood," said Ben.

When he walked towards the back door, he was confronted by Sam. "Dad," he began, "can I ask you something?"

Ben was curious and replied, "Sure, son."

The teenager looked seemingly disgusted at his father and asked, "Why do you always give Mrs. Wilson money when you know that's what she comes for? Mom told us that your work has slowed down and that we have to be careful."

That comment struck a nerve with Ben. Without hesitation he lost all facial expression and looked straight at his son. In a stern voice he said, "Sometimes we all need a little help." The father stormed outside in a fury to get the firewood. Sam's ride was waiting for him out in front. He left digesting his father's response.

Soon the living room was rich with the crackling of a fire and the aroma of spiced tea. Sharon craved the attention she was getting from Ben and Gloria. This compelled the old woman to tell stories about her childhood one after another, after another...

Several cups of tea and a few logs later Ben noticed the time. It was getting close to nine o'clock and almost time for *his shift*. He politely drew attention to the living room clock and expressed that he had an appointment at the fellowship hall that night.

"I am afraid that I have to leave," apologized Ben.

Looking towards the wall that held the brass time piece, Sharon became excited. "Oh!" she exclaimed. "I need to get home and feed my Nightingale. She must be starving by now."

Ben capitalized on the moment by saying, "I'll walk you home on the way to the hall. Besides, it's icy outside and I don't want you to take a chance on falling."

Sharon gave her undivided attention to Ben while nodding her head.

The old woman finished her tea and placed it on the matching small plate that lay on the stand next to her. Placing the empty cup on the plate, she turned to Ben and Gloria. "Thank you for such a pleasant evening," she said in an appreciative tone.

Holding her purse, the independent senior was still able to get up from the chair and follow Ben to the front door. The host already had her coat open for her and all she had to do was turn around and extend her arms. Like a duo in ballet, the coat systematically draped over her body in one motion.

Sharon opened her purse to put her matching pink gloves and hat back on. By the time she was finished, Ben was already dressed for the walk. He wore a stylish brown leather western jacket and an 'Indiana Jones' hat.

With arm in arm, the would-be mother and son team left the warm home to brave the frosty evening. The strong man cautiously took small steps to stabilize his cargo. He stared down at the old woman's feet and safely guided her. The senior who lived alone possessed a sense of security; she knew that she was protected and felt that she belonged.

"Watch your step," cautioned Ben.

"I promise I will," vowed Sharon Wilson.

The length of the two properties seemed to take an eternity to travel. Finally, they stood at her front door. "I want to thank you so much for everything," remarked the widow.

"The pleasure's mine," said Ben. "Just promise me that you will always let me know if you need anything, and that includes visiting us at any time." Ben meant what he said and knew that Sharon understood it.

"I promise to let you know if I ever need anything," she said in relief. Sharon reached into her purse and pulled out her keys. It took a minute for the trembling gloved hand to find the keyhole. She found her mark, slid the key in, and turned it, opening the door to find her 10-year-old calico cat patiently waiting for her.

"Meow, meow," greeted the cat.

"Nightingale!" cried out Sharon. "You must be hungry; let mommy feed you now." The old lady entered her home.

Ben was happy to see that she had a loved one waiting for her. "You two have a good evening," he said with all his charm.

"Oh, we will," answered Sharon. "Thank you for the wonderful evening. You be careful out there," she advised.

"Don't worry about me," laughed Ben. "Good night, Mrs. Wilson."

"Good night, Ben," she said as she closed the door and locked it.

Ben felt *right*. His humble neighbor was a vulnerable old lady that he *knew* was assigned to him. He thanked God for being the one chosen to live close to her.

It was now time to continue his evening. The Good Samaritan walked down the path that led to the ice-packed sidewalk. Taking a sharp left, he continued his trek to the fellowship hall. Looking at his watch he saw that he had the needed fifteen minutes to arrive on time and relieve the shivering comrade waiting for him.

It would soon be Ben Skates disguised as a hobo holding the sign that begged for mercy. While his family would be sleeping at home, *dad* would be slowly freezing on a street corner.

A necessary evil needed to survive...

Chapter 11

SNOW BANKS FEEDING A brisk northern wind forced everyone to stay home another night. The wind, however, seemed to subside whenever Ben walked outside. For whatever reason, it aided him when he escorted his neighbor home and stayed with him while he walked to his fellowship hall. This guaranteed him the tranquility needed to nurture the stress and anxiety that plagued his life. The family man who was looking for work could now relax, think, and pray uninterrupted. Ben was now alone...almost.

It was a walk down memory lane. His first landmark was a faded bleach-white house that he used to attend birthday parties in. In fact, his best childhood friend still lived in this rustic two story home: Mike Talbot. Many times, they camped out in the backyard and counted stars. They even went to high school together and won the state title in baseball their senior year.

Ben giggled to himself, remembering the harmless pranks they did. The mischievous side needed for a small town boy to create excitement had arisen a few times. This was the horseplay that fathers had to discipline and later laugh about in the barber shop. Ben chuckled as he passed Mike's house.

Several doors down was a crystal field where one of the county's oldest structures stood. This was where his mother used to walk him to every morning and pick him up from every afternoon. It was the elementary school he attended many years ago. Powdered snow outlined the vintage swing set, monkey bars, and volleyball poles where he used to play. The two story brick building still held its integrity despite being over seventy years old. It was deemed sacred because all of his friends and living relatives were alumni.

Many of Ben's fondest childhood memories spawned here. As a little boy, his favorite class was art. The loving son would take his time meticulously painting, sculpting, and building creations. With pride, he would run to his mother when school let out and present her his latest Picasso. The mother lived out her life surrounded by Ben's masterpieces.

Down one block and across the street was Miner High School. A more modern building replaced the old one, but the campus had been relatively untouched, resembling the days when he wore his letterman's sweater. What was important to Ben was that the baseball field was original. The nostalgic bleachers and scoreboard were positioned like a page out of yesterday. The blanket of snow covered the family legacy. It was on that very mound that Ben's father and son pitched a no-hitter, just as he once did; a state record never to be equaled. With pride, Ben Skates passed the diamond with his chest puffed out.

He remembered the immortal words that his father once told him, words of wisdom that he passed on to his son: "baseball teaches life."

The glory days of the past dissipated with each step. The domino theory of a depressed community would now come into light. A tiny red house appeared next. It was the home of Cliff Hammond, a friend that he had worked with for years. Cliff was feeling the economic crunch as hard as anyone. He was married with four children and had been out of work longer than Ben. "I hope to God that Cliff can survive," he muttered.

Ben continued his travels.

A boarded up convenient store was a sign of the times. The loss of local jobs and families moving far away pushed the crippled small business into closure. It was one of many that couldn't survive any longer.

Several more houses were passed. Some had 'For Sale' signs hanging from a wooden post just off the sidewalk. Those that were occupied had smoke venting through the chimney with the drapes closed. The tracks from their vehicles were buried from the snow flurry that fell days ago. The thickness of undisturbed snow evenly covered their cars and rooftops.

Walking another block displayed a deeper blow. It was the empty lot of a used car dealership with only its small wooden office remaining. Next door was the *coup-dye-grace*. It was 'Ace's' abandoned fenced-in supply yard where Ben used to work. This business helped supply the county with all of its highway supplies ranging from asphalt equipment to sewage pipes. The state cut backs forced this surplus lot to close. All work was now consolidated on their second lot near the edge of town; a forced tactic that reduced every man down to twenty hours a week.

The town of Miner was slowly dying. The dwindling community resembled a checkerboard with open doors alternating vacated ones.

By default, a new card was recently put into the deck. The fuel pumps for the state vehicles were purchased by an independent fueling company and automated for public use. This greatly impaired the age-old gas station in the neighboring town, but did provide a hint of a silver lining in the exchange.

The out of state oil company placed a lone sign on the freeway going both directions that advertised fuel and a local cafe. The town of Miner was now on the map.

This gave their humble community a ray of hope by calling out to unknown travelers. It would inadvertently bring potential clientele down Main Street who needed fuel. From there, it would be displayed that the town of Miner had some merit.

'Charlie's Bowling Alley' was still in operation with a bar attached to it. 'Beth's Café' was open every day from breakfast to dinner and 'Ella's Coffee Shop' was a popular hangout that also served as a malt shop known for its great pizza. 'Eli's General Store' carried much needed hardware, appliances, and apparel. In the heart of the town with one traffic light was 'The Miner Grocery Store'. A Laundromat, gift shop, and two second-hand stores filled in some of the cracks.

This brought hope that some might sit down for a meal, shop, or even see a house that they could afford. What it did guarantee was that all would have to travel past Elm Street to exit the town... and see Elmo.

Ben continued his walk. The road gradually curved downhill exposing what remained of Miner. Four blocks were dimly lit by staggered streetlights and the shops were all closed except for the bar at Charlie's.

Ben squinted his eyes two blocks past the traffic light. He looked at the far corner before the town's only freeway ramp. There stood a silhouette holding a sign the size of a dinner tray. Its breath dissipated in an upward direction as the lonesome figure swayed side to side in a futile attempt to stay warm. The black bold print on the cardboard sign was almost readable from where Ben was. It was a fellow member of 'The Men of Miner Fellowship Hall' that was scavenging for handouts. An ally of Ben's soon to be relieved of duty.

A car with out of state license plates passed Ben. It was obviously a family that needed gas. Ben held his breath as the vehicle stopped at the red light, allowing the beggar to be in plain sight. Ben said a prayer hoping that the travelers would show compassion and give. The light turned green, the brake lights vanished, and the car slowly accelerated forward. The disguised figure positioned the sign towards the car as it approached. Like most, the vehicle gained speed and left the small town.

Ben could sense the dejection his *brother* felt. He picked up his pace and within minutes, met with his hall member. A close look at the man's weary blue eyes made identification easy. It was Wilson Thomas, a shivering 60-year-old.

In shame, he gave his report. "I didn't get a thing," said the quivering man. "Not even one red cent."

"That's okay," said Ben in a comforting voice. "At least you tried. Maybe I'll have better luck."

Looking at his worn out friend he said, "Let's get you inside. You're overdue for a cup of soup."

"That sounds good to me," replied Wilson.

Ben took the sign out of Wilson's hand and put his arm around him. Together they limped to the building across the street.

Chapter III

THE OLDEST BUILDING IN town was the Samson Building off of Elm Street. It was made of brick and stood three stories high. In its heyday, the building was a department store with offices and apartments. Today, it appears condemned and only housed 'The Men of Miner Fellowship Hall.'

This was a food bank and soup kitchen where men gathered for prayer and goodwill. When necessary, it also served as a shelter for the homeless. These good souls took it upon themselves to make a difference. What government funding couldn't provide, they found a way. Anyone in need knew to go to the fellowship hall.

Ben marched Wilson down the frozen sidewalk that outlined the vintage building. Like a slum, the first two doors were boarded up with the traditional 'no trespassing' signs stapled to them. The third door was the last breath of life for this neglected monument. It was still in use with a plate of glass next to it that had 'The Men of Miner Fellowship Hall' painted in antique gold with black trim.

If one peered through the window, they would see a dusty old room that had long wooden benches paired with matching tables.

At first glance it could pass for a monastery. A closer look displayed faded yellow walls with pictures and portraits randomly hung. To the very front was a stage that held a podium. What was more important was the brass urn placed in front of it. This was for donations to keep the hall in operation and to help as many families as possible. On the wall behind the stage was a large American flag perfectly centered.

The men inside resembled retirees passing time in a barber shop. They were sitting in front of their coffee cups visiting with friends. Others were huddled off to the side playing cards.

Ben opened the door and placed the tattered sign on the nearest table. Wilson was like a fatigued prizefighter that went the distance. He could barely walk as he entered the room with Ben's assistance. Those seated immediately got up. A chair was positioned for Wilson in front of a portable heater.

He started to take off the cold leather gloves, hat and ski mask and placed them next to the sign. His pasty white clean-shaven face was revealed with wild gray hair standing up from static.

"Sorry guys," said Wilson as he lowered his head. "I came up empty tonight." He was flocked by the members receiving a well-deserved pat on the back.

A bent figure with a cane hobbled up to Wilson, confronting him. It was Red Pennington, the town's oldest citizen. His intense blue eyes peered through a weathered face that survived the Great Depression. "That's okay," said Red. The feisty old man continued, "We've survived these times before and will again." He winked and returned to his card game. Wilson paused for a moment feeling encouraged. It was now time to get warm.

Trebling outstretched hands reached to the heater as he leaned forward. Slowly, he moved each finger one by one, allowing the medicating heat to revive them. The trench coat with extra room came off next. This uncovered a blue long-sleeve sweat shirt that provided additional insulation for the boney frame. The coat was draped next to the hat and leather gloves.

Wilson sat down in the chair waiting for him. Bending over, he took off the oversized shoes, handing them to Ben. He stood back up and peeled off the baggy pants that belonged in a vaudeville show, having worn gray sweatpants underneath.

"It's a good thing that I wore my sweats," he commented. "That's what saved me out there." He handed the hobo pants to Ben's waiting hands. Wilson sat down again. This time he leaned back and extended his rigid legs. The tired man made a long sigh of relief as he rested his numb stocking feet inches away from the heater.

A hot cup of chicken noodle soup was handed to him. "Gee," he said in a pleasant tone. "This is just like home."

The room laughed as someone added, "This *is* home." Laughter elevated with members looking at one another in agreement.

"I better get out there," said Ben. He took off his hat and jacket, placing them on the open arms of the coat rack. Sitting down on the edge of a bench next to Wilson, he removed his shoes, sliding them under the rack. It was now his turn to wear the 'one-size-fits-all' Santa suit.

Wilson extended his left arm and tapped his fingers on Ben's chest. "I suggest that you fill up on soup first," he advised. "It's freezing out there."

"That sounds good," responded Ben. The big man left for the kitchen and returned with a steaming cup. He sat down in the same chair and savored it while he thought. Finally, he turned around and asked those present a question. "Do any of our families know about this?"

The room stood quiet as if everyone was waiting for someone to speak up first. After a brief pause, Wilson spoke. Looking straight ahead with a blank stare he calmly said, "I don't know."

Gene Fletcher, a middle-aged African American, commented next. The married man with two daughters in grade school had something to say. "I don't think that our families know that we are the ones who are actually begging out there. They seem to trust that we do a good job watching over this town and that we would keep a close eye over something like that." Scanning the room he added. "And they're right."

"I hope you're right," replied Ben in a soft tone. "I don't want our families to know the fears we're hiding." On that note he finished his soup and started to dress into the hobo outfit. Once dressed, the respected man walked by the table that held the cardboard sign and picked it up. With determination, he went outside to man his post.

It was now twenty minutes past nine as the packed snow crunched underneath his feet. Ben crossed the street and reached the desolate corner that was littered with matching footprints. Standing tall, he looked at the lone freeway ramp. This was the only place where blessings could arrive. It allowed strangers to enter the hidden poverty-stricken community they called *home*.

The barren road was a layer of ice that reflected headlights entering town. This aided the cause by illuminating the corner they stood on when cars returned to the freeway. This momentarily gave one the illusion that they were performing on a grand stage, a necessary act for the starving artist. The last chance to believe in a man with dignity trying to survive.

Tonight Ben Skates was that man.

A mild breeze gently combed the town of Miner. The slight rustling of dried leaves, twigs, and a trace of litter glided across Main Street. These graceful movements of nature would entertain

Ben as he talked to God and prayed for a Good Samaritan to pass through town.

Ben's somber moment was interrupted. A car could faintly be heard off in the distance. Looking at the exit ramp, he saw approaching headlights grow larger and larger. Finally, a dark four door car appeared at the bottom of the ramp and stopped at the sign. It was the only vehicle on the road and proceeded with caution. Ben moved towards the curve and displayed the sign towards the moving vehicle.

This wasn't a disappointment yet because it was on the opposite side of the street. Ben was aware that the driver could only be here for one reason: to get gas. In moments, the car would have to pass a second time in the lane closest to him. This would allow the driver ample time to access the situation and hopefully his conscious.

Ben patiently waited and prayed. "Dear God, please let that driver be more fortunate than us and willing to give."

What seemed like an hour was only ten minutes. The driver did return having to stop at the traffic light and further study the panhandler. When the light turned green Ben held the sign up at an angle to be more easily read. The stranger drove past him with increasing speed and left the small town.

Ben was disappointed but held on to his faith. He continued to stand on the icy 'no-man's land' as the fierce cold slowly penetrated his body. His chilled fingers were losing dexterity. Breathing heavily, swaying, and marching in place generated body heat in a losing battle. Seconds inched along and became minutes. The dead of winter controlled the night with everything at a frozen stand-still. All was quiet as Ben peered down the empty street that glowed under the lamps.

Looking past the meager business district, he panned over the hill where he lived. He thought about his beautiful wife and the day they planned to have a family. Never in his wildest dreams could he ever see himself as a bum holding a sign at the edge of town. *She's must be getting tired of me spending hours at the hall every night*, he thought to himself.

His son and daughter came to mind. Their faces always lit up when he came home from work. They eagerly told him of their day in school and what they wanted to be when they grew up. The future model and baseball star loved the strength their father gave them. He taught them to always be independent and to believe in themselves.

Tears ran down the face of the proud beggar.

A faint pulsating rumbling sound broke the tranquility. It was the unmistakable call of a diesel engine downshifting. A mighty eighteen wheeler was slowing down to enter the town of Miner. Two beams of light hit the center of the street that faced the ramp. Their intensity grew as a patriotic red, white, and blue semi slowly rolled into view and stopped. Its air brakes discharged a powerful releasing sound as the cross country courier crawled forward and turned left on Main Street.

Ben was like a boy watching the circus come to town. He marveled at the gigantic vehicle with chrome wheels and wondered where it came from and where it was going. An adventure that beckoned to Ben and his friends throughout their childhood whenever a truck pulled into town.

A toot from the mighty horn acknowledged the castaway as he frantically waved back. Contact had been established with Ben's hopes coming alive.

Squinting his eyes he read 'Smith Trucking' printed in red on the blue and white door. His excitement grew as he watched the truck advance down Main Street through the green light. The freighter signaled left and turned to the automated pumps. He looked up to the starry night and prayed to God for a generous handout.

His prayer would soon be answered.

Forty-five minutes later the Kenworth left the fuel pumps and returned towards the man holding the sign. The truck stopped at the red traffic signal and released its breaks when the light changed. The headlights shut on and off twice to alert Ben as it drove up to him and stopped.

The window rolled down with a driver team inside. A closer look saw a pair of 'Smiths' sitting inside wearing uniforms that matched the truck. They were defined by obvious family traits. Manicured thin brown hair and blue eyes gave distinction to their handsome lean faces. The image was further enhanced with the charm of southern hospitality. The man sitting closest to Ben spoke first. "We have some coffee and an extra sandwich," he said in a polite tone. "We'd feel very honored if you would accept this." He proceeded to hand him a small brown paper bag accompanied with a tall Styrofoam cup capped with a white plastic lid.

It was like manna from heaven as Ben reached towards the cab and accepted the gifts. He bent over and placed them on the frozen ground. Standing up he looked at the tandem. "Thank you," he said in a shivering voice. "Thank you so much for caring for me."

The driver leaned over and looked at the masked man. He immediately sensed the goodness he was made up of. Reaching into his wallet he said, "We also want you to have this." He removed two twenty dollar bills and handed it to his partner who passed the currency through the window. Ben reached and took the money. "Sir," said the driver, "We know that you have no choice but to be here." With sincerity he continued, "Your luck will change and you'll do just fine. I just wish that we could do more for you."

Ben shook with emotion saying, "You have done more than enough for me! I will pray to God and thank Him for bringing you to me. God bless both of you and thank you so much for your kindness."

"You are quite welcome," said the passenger. The duo gave Ben a thumbs up. Rolling up the window, they continued their journey.

"Thank you!" yelled Ben as the semi shifted gears. A farewell toot was given as the crusaders entered the ramp and disappeared. He listened to his heroes gain speed and fade into the night. Ben looked at the bills and put them into his coat pocket. He was rejuvenated knowing that there were those out there that still cared.

Standing motionless, he bowed and said a prayer of gratitude. Once finished, Ben took off his gloves and placed them in his coat pocket. Lifting the ski mask up to his forehead he squatted down and picked up the coffee. Removing the lid released an aroma of steam that dissipated around him. He took a sip and realized that it was adequately hot along with being a very rich coffee. He took another sip and quickly put the plastic lid back on. He placed the coffee back on the ice and picked up the paper bag. Ben stood up and looked inside. Seeing the wrapped sandwich, he realized how hungry he was. With numb fingers, he pulled it out of the sack. It felt like a hand warmer.

Ben was aware that the good men thoughtfully microwaved the meal in their home on wheels. Meticulously, he unwrapped the end facing him. Lifting a corner of rye bread a pastrami sandwich was exposed, further tantalizing the hungry man. Using both hands, he leaned over and took a bite. It was the most delicious meal he'd ever tasted. He held the warm sandwich close to his mouth and savored it.

Ben's spirits had been lifted. The generosity from the truckers gave him hope that others would follow. Several more vehicles quietly passed through town only to pretend that they didn't see the man on the corner.

Finally, a car slowed down with the passenger window lowered. A young woman took careful aim and gently tossed a fist full of loose change from a safe distance. Ben realized that he was viewed as an otter being thrown a fish. He still expressed gratitude with a friendly wave. The shiny coins slid in all directions. He combed the area over and over again recovering a total of three dollars and forty-seven cents. He placed the coins in his empty coffee container.

His shift was almost over when one last vehicle stopped to donate. It was an elderly woman with license plates two states away. She was confident and very personal. "I hope that this helps you," said the regal looking gray haired woman. Ben nodded as he held his hand out inches under hers. She lowered her hand touching his glove and placed three dollars in his palm.

"Thank you very much," he said with a hoarse voice behind the mask.

"You are quite welcome," came her reply. She rolled up the window and drove away. He watched the woman that he never met before and would probably never see again drive onto the freeway ramp and continue her life. Again, Ben felt blessed.

It was getting close to one o'clock in the morning. He looked down Elm Street towards the entrance of the fellowship hall. A figure came out of the front door and motioned him to return. It was the changing of the guards and not a minute too soon. Ben's feet were cold. In fact, they were so cold that he could barely walk. He would return successful though, having collected forty-six dollars and forty-seven cents for the hall. The weary man had quite a night as God graced him with good souls. He would enter the hall, place the money in the brass urn, change clothing, and stay just long enough to get warm.

Then he would walk home to resume his *other* life...

Chapter IV

THE WALK HOME GAVE Ben time to reflect on the strangers that helped him that night. He realized that they all came from families just as he did. He also understood that like himself, they too would have problems of their own. Still, they reached out to him and gave. This inspired him to help others even further.

With keys in hand, he walked up the steps that led to his front door. It was two o'clock in the morning with only the porch light on. He quietly unlocked the door, entered the warm home, and turned on the entry way light. Next, he gently closed the door behind him and locked it. He placed his hat and coat on the coat rack next to the door then slowly turned around. The walls all held pictures of his family that seemed to be staring at him.

More concerns came into focus as he looked at each expression. His daughter needed money to get glamor shots done for a modeling agency and his son was due for a new baseball glove. The last thing Ben wanted to be guilty of was to let up on the dreams his children had. Money however, would be the deciding factor. His savings account was almost depleted and the unemployment benefits from his job would expire in two months. He even owed money to a friend.

The responsible father was doing everything he could think of. He was now walking instead of driving within town. Ben cut more corners by secretively eating less at home and allowing the soup kitchen at the fellowship hall to subsidize meals. When allowed, he accepted food from the food bank to take home. The provider was in constant search to find any odd job at any price. The rational father subtlety got his children involved by having them 'brown-bagging it' to school, just in case the day ever came when things got worse.

The pictures of his wife showed smiles of unconditional love. The same smile she always had whenever she looked at him. Gloria knew that he was hiding how bad things actually were. She also knew that he was doing his very best and would never fail them. The supportive wife never complained and rarely asked for anything. She only wanted to have a family with Ben and stay with him. *I am such a lucky man,* he thought to himself.

Ben would finish up his long day with a hot bath followed by much needed sleep.

The breakfast table signified the start of another day. Gloria served hot oatmeal with milk, brown sugar, bananas, and raisins. A plate centered the table, holding a stack of buttered toast with homemade blackberry jam. Hot chocolate, orange juice and coffee made the 'wake-up' meal complete.

Gloria sat down across from Ben as hands stretched out for grace. Once all hands were held, the family bowed as Ben led the prayer.

"Dear Lord, we are grateful for this meal. We thank you for this wonderful family and the home we live in. Please bless our day."

"Amen," responded the table. Hands released with all looking at one another. Spoons were grabbed and ladled into the hot cereal.

Gloria instantaneously initiated a conversation by asking everyone how they slept.

"Fine, mom," responded Susan.

"I slept real good," said Sam.

"I was probably asleep before my head hit the pillow," said Ben laughingly. "I don't have to ask how you slept," he said to Gloria. "You were sound asleep and didn't even hear me when I got in bed."

Looking towards his children he asked, "Anything special going on today?"

Susan spoke first. "I have an exam today in history, but I'm ready for it." Her facial expressions suddenly grew into excitement as she had more to say. "After school I will be going to the auditorium for a career seminar about modeling." The young beauty looked at her mom.

"Well good," said Gloria. "The world's waiting for you!"

Sam talked next. "I don't have much going on today at school." The son leaned over and ate another mouthful of oatmeal. Once finished he look at his dad and expressed a cagy grin. "I will be busy after school though," he said. "Coach Jenkins is taking some of us to the batting cage. He is going to introduce us to some people and time our fastballs in front of them."

Ben leaned back in his chair, beaming at his son. He knew that for a coach to access a select few players during the off season could only mean one thing: they were being promoted for scholarships. He winked at Sam and nodded his head. *They* knew what this meant.

The teenage boy would now ask his dad a question. "Dad, since it's Friday, can I hang out with Ryan and the guys later? We were thinking about going out for pizza or something."

"That's fine," answered the father. "I trust that you guys will stay out of trouble."

"You don't have to worry about us," assured Sam.

Breakfast was eventually finished with two voices saying, "That was good, mom. Thanks!" The high school students excused themselves from the table and ran upstairs. Moments later they ran back down fully dressed with books in hand. Gloria handed her son and daughter their lunches as they scrambled to the door. "Bye mom and dad," cried out Sam as he left the home.

"Bye, mom and dad," yelled Susan as she followed her brother, closing the door behind her.

The parents had no time to respond. With opened mouths they stared at the closed door and slowly turned to each other with dumbfounded expressions. Seeing the humor in what just happened they broke into laughter and hugged.

Gloria was aware that her husband's job could only offer him three days of work. Today, being Friday, meant that they would have some time together. "I'll pour us another cup of coffee," she said kissing Ben on the cheek. They walked to the kitchen table and Ben sat down.

Gloria poured coffee into Ben's cup and topped hers off. No sooner did she sit down than the cell phone on the table rang. Ben was within arm's reach and picked it up. "Hello," he answered with a masculine voice.

A saintly tone responded. "Good morning, Ben, this is Troy." To his surprise it was Troy Meeker, Ben's best friend.

"Troy," called out Ben. "It's great to hear from you!"

"Well, it's good to hear you too," he reciprocated. "Ben, the reason why I am calling is because I have a job today that will pay two men. I thought that you and I could spend the day together and earn some money, if you're not busy."

The offer was music to Ben's ears because he was in desperate need for work. This God-send went beyond supporting his family; it would also maintain his identity of being a proud working man. What made things even better was that he would be working with the man he carried the most respect for: Troy Meeker. "That sounds great!" replied Ben.

"I thought you'd be interested," said Troy. The compassionate deacon began to explain the situation. "The Carltons are the oldest couple in town with a house that's poorly insulated. They called me this morning in a state of panic to let me know that their water pipes froze last night. They offered to pay me what they could to get their water running again. I know that you and I can get this done in one day."

"You're right," agreed Ben, "I know where they live and I'd be happy to help them."

"I knew you would," said Troy in a jubilant voice. He elaborated further on the day's project. "Our church storage has a surplus of insulation that includes tape for pipes. I was given permission to use the materials on their house. We also have a torch we can use to thaw out the pipes before we tape them. After that we can go as far as we can insulating the house."

"That sounds good to me," said Ben.

"I'll get the materials in my van and meet you at their house in an hour," said Troy.

"I'll be there," said Ben. Raising his voice slightly he gave one last comment. "I appreciate this, Troy."

"That's quite alright," he replied. Troy hung up as Ben placed his cell phone on the table.

Ben looked at Gloria knowing that she heard the one-sided conversation. "Honey," he said with a smug look. "I'd love to spend the day with you but I have a job to go to."

Gloria could see the esteem in Ben's eyes and hugged her man with both hands. "I'll fill your lunch box with enough food for you and Troy," she said. "You'll also have a thermos full of hot coffee with an extra cup."

"Thanks, Gloria," he said patting her on the back. "I'll get ready now." Ben let go of his wife and went upstairs to dress for the cold day. Gloria cheerfully started to brew more coffee and began to make sandwiches.

Within a half hour Ben was at the front door dressed in his work clothes with lunchbox in hand. He gazed at Gloria and kissed her goodbye. "Bye, honey," said the supportive wife. "Have a good day and tell Troy I say hello."

"I will," said Ben, "and thanks for taking care of us." Like the two children before him, Ben left the house to greet the day.

His travels were pleasantly interrupted when he walked in front of Mrs. Wilson's house. The old widow peeled back a corner of the maroon drapes that enclosed her living room. She was peering out the window and frantically waving to get Ben's attention.

Ben looked over and saw her. Then he noticed something. In one hand was the familiar air-tight container that always held her famous chocolate chip cookies. The see-through plastic revealed that it was jammed-packed with her mouthwatering cookies. The child came out in Ben as he smiled and rubbed his stomach. She was pleased that he knew what awaited him. The woman left the window and in seconds started to open the front door as Ben walked up her path.

The door opened with Sharon Wilson wearing a pink bathrobe. Her cat stood next to her looking up at Ben with mystical eyes.

"I baked these especially for you," said the thoughtful old lady as she handed the container to Ben. "I know that you will see many people today and share them."

Ben was touched. He knew that his neighbor slowed down with age and must have spent hours baking the cookies. It was truly a labor of love. "Why, Mrs. Wilson," commented Ben in a soft voice, "You will never know how many people have enjoyed your cookies. They are just one of a kind." He held the gift with both hands, staring down at it. Looking up with the compassion of Father Murphy he humbly said, "Thank you."

"I am glad that you like them," said the thoughtful senior. "I have to close the door now, it's getting cold. Have a good day, Ben."

"Have a good day too, Mrs. Wilson," he answered. Sharon Wilson closed the door and locked it. Ben left her property and walked to the Carlton's bearing a gift. He was within one block of the job site when a horn honked behind him. It was the church's white utility van slowly driving past with Troy waving. Ben smiled and waved back. Troy drove a few houses down and parked in front of the elder couple's house.

Ben was soon standing in front of the faded green house with no running water. Troy opened the back of the van and walked up to Ben extending his hand. "I'm glad you're here with me today," said Troy with a happy face.

"The pleasure's all mine," quipped Ben as they shook hands.

"Let's visit with Mr. and Mrs. Carlton and see what's ailing them," suggested Troy. The men walked to the front door with blistered white paint and knocked.

Over two minutes passed and then the front door slowly opened. A trembling old man with a walker answered the door. This was the home of Chester Carlton. He was dressed in slacks with a sleeveless t-shirt. He was all of five feet four inches, weighing close to one-hundred pounds. Thin gray hair covered the sides of his head. Blue eyes peered through wire-rimmed bifocals as he positioned himself for better vision. "Glad you could make it, Troy," greeted the retired military man. "Please come in." The 90-year-old moved backwards, opening the door further. He turned around and cautiously strolled with the walker to his easy chair. Sitting next to him was his wife of sixty-eight years, Marian. The petite gray haired woman sat on the sofa wearing a blue and white dress that almost touched the floor. Her walker stood faithfully next to her. "Please sit down," said Chester.

Troy entered first as Ben closed the door behind him. They sat down on the vacant chairs facing the couple. There was silence as the visitors studied their antique surroundings. The room had portraits in lavish frames with lamps dating back over seventy years. The room opened at one end displaying a dining room. A matching oak table with tall chairs was paired with an oak china closet from the turn of the century. Directly above hung a crystal chandler that held cobwebs. Dust overtook where the old couple could no longer reach.

In front of the couple was a coffee table. It was littered with old magazines and an envelope from the electric company marked 'final notice.'

Ben understood that Troy also noticed the delinquent bill as their eyes met.

"We'd offer you something to eat," said Chester in a humble voice, "but we don't have anything."

Ben spoke up. "I brought lunch for everyone. I hope that ham sandwiches, coffee, carrots and chocolate chip cookies are acceptable."

Marian gave an immediate response. "That will be the best meal we've had in months."

Ben put his lunch box on the table. "We can eat in the dining room," said Chester.

Ben and Troy watched the seniors grab onto their walkers and slowly stand up. They led the way to the dining room table. "I'll get some plates and silverware," said Marian.

Troy interrupted. "Let me get them and you two can sit down."

"Thank you, Troy," said the wife. "You'll find them in the cabinet and drawer next to the sink."

In a reassuring voice Troy said, "Don't worry, I'll find them." He walked through the opening that led to the kitchen. What he saw frightened him. It was the original kitchen from when the house was built almost seventy years ago. Outdated white appliances cried out to be replaced. Vintage pink and black tile counter tops with a matching linoleum floor stood the test of time. The fixtures showed rust. Troy had to look into their refrigerator. It was almost empty with a partial carton of milk accompanied with vegetables and a pot of spaghetti. *Thank God I found out about this,* thought the deacon.

He knew that Ben would want to see how this elderly couple was living. "Hey, Ben," called out Troy in a pleasant voice, "can you help me for a moment?"

Ben stared at Chester and Marian with a smile. He stood up and excused himself from the table.

Once entering the kitchen he saw Troy raise his arms upwards and slowly turn around in the kitchen of yesterday. Nothing had to be said. Troy opened the refrigerator as Ben walked to it and bent over to get a good look. "I will go to the fellowship hall and get some groceries for them after lunch," said Troy. Ben remained quiet and nodded his head in agreement. Only two plate settings were brought back.

Ben explained the situation. "Troy and I just ate and only brought lunch for you two."

"That's right," said Troy.

"Oh, how thoughtful of you," replied Marian. "We are out of water right now," she added. "But, we do have some milk if you would like."

"That's quite alright," said Troy.

Ben opened his lunch box and placed a sandwich on each plate. Next, he put a few carrot stems with each and said, "And we also brought you coffee with your cups right here." He opened his thermos and poured steaming coffee into the mugs he brought.

The couple twitched with excitement as the plates were decorated and placed in front of them. Chester looked at Troy and said, "Marian and I would be honored if you would lead us in grace."

The deacon was honored. "Why, I'd love to," he said. At that moment all held hands and leaned forward. Troy masterfully thanked the Lord for that moment and for the welfare for the Carltons and for everyone in the entire community. Once finished all released hands and sat up. Chester and his wife looked at one another in anticipation and began to eat.

Troy and Ben watched them slowly take a bite of a sandwich and lean back in delight.

"And for desert, we have chocolate chip cookies," reminded Troy.

Chester and Marian's excitement continued to grow. They were now acting like children that were being rewarded for good behavior. Troy and Ben watched as the former teenagers took turns giggling at each other with their mouths full. The little charades they did and how they cleverly amused one another continued to entertained Ben and Troy. It was obvious that they were still in love; now more than ever.

A conversation soon arose that included the visitors. An hour of laughter passed by within minutes. Lunch was finally over with Ben and Troy clearing the table and washing the dishes. It was now time to access the chore ahead of them.

Ben volunteered to fix the water pipes. Troy would inspect the crawl space under the house and the attic. He would staple insulation everywhere needed until he ran out of material. But first, he would go to the fellowship hall and get a care package.

Ben spoke to Chester and told him to have the faucet in the bathtub opened. The old man followed his instructions while Ben went outside to brave the cold.

Ben aggressively went to work by utilizing the portable butane torch Troy brought. He continuously applied an open flame to the frozen pipes that were exposed outside. From the water main in front of the house to the pipes that left the frozen ground that entered the dwelling, he swept the intense flame on them. Taking a shovel, he dug around the pipes that exited from the ground. He concentrated the flame on the junction that was underground. Soon the damp pipes slightly shook as the sound of running water could be heard.

Ben continued to massage the exposed pipes with the dancing torch. He looked towards the living room window and saw what he needed to see. The Carltons were leaning against their walkers giving Ben a thumbs up. They were celebrating that they had running water. Ben raised his free hand, signaling an okay sign with his fingers.

Troy returned and left his van carrying two bags of groceries. The man who was taking care of his mother was on a mission and would not fail the aging couple. Chester and his wife saw Troy with the bags and opened their door. The couple was astounded as Troy gave a graceful presentation. "The Men of Minor Fellowship Hall would like you to accept this as a gift. May I please come in and put these in your kitchen?"

The cavalry had arrived at the Carlton home. Not only was their house being winterized for the season, but they were also being supplied with the most valuable commodity needed to survive: food.

"Please come in," said Chester.

Troy entered the house and was escorted to the kitchen. Placing the groceries on the counter he looked at the enlightened couple and spoke. "The hall always has food whenever you need any. Just let me know and I'll get you some."

The good man changed subjects. "I brought some insulation for your home. I need to do a quick inspection throughout the house to see where it's needed the most."

Chester placed his hand on Troy's shoulder and said, "You can do whatever you need to do."

Troy applied his humor by reciprocating with a military stance and saying, "Yes, sir!" He saluted the couple and left the kitchen to access the house.

Chester and Marian stood in awe. They marveled at the man of God as he continued to serve them. Next they looked at the grocery bags and began to empty their contents. There was more than donated food. It was obvious that Troy took money out of his own pocket and added to the gift with a few store bought items. Coffee, milk, steaks, canned food, and bread were just some of the items. Wide-eyed, they starred at one another in disbelief.

Troy walked upstairs to the attic. What he saw didn't surprise him. He discovered that the attic ceiling was exposed wood from the frame that supported the roof. The heat from the house would escape through the roof. The task of using a staple gun to hang insulation in place would take hardly any time at all. He went outside and viewed the crawl space under the house to see the same conditions.

He reported the situation to Ben and let him know that he could quickly fasten insulation on the bare frames. Ben let him know that the water was already running and that he would now tape the exposed pipes. Once finished, he'd work on the attic.

The frail couple watched the men labor like children watching a construction site. They were intrigued as they watched Troy slide under their house with his staple gun, light, and bales of insulation. Soon a rapid tap-tap-tap sound came from under the house. It traveled from one corner to another as the handyman covered ground. It would stop when Troy had to go to the van to get more rolls. He would immediately return and maintain his frantic pace.

Troy completed the undercarriage of the house just as Ben finished his assignment. "I think we have enough for the attic," said Troy. "I have an extra staple gun in the van if you want to help."

"I'll get it and bring what's left of the insulation," said Ben.

With determination, they went upstairs to the attic and quickly blanketed the wooden beams. There was a partial roll left of insulation when they finished. "I'll put it back in the van with the tools," said Troy. "I'll meet you downstairs and we can visit with the Carltons."

"Okay," said Ben.

The tools and materials were all put away with the van locked. Troy tapped on the front door and entered to sit down with Ben, Chester, and Marian.

Once they were all seated, Chester pulled out his wallet and said, "I don't have much, but it's all yours."

"Put that away," ordered Ben. "We didn't come here to charge you for anything. We just wanted to visit and see if there was anything that we could do for you."

Chester was speechless. He couldn't believe their generosity and quivered with his mouth wide open. Troy was impressed. He knew that Ben worked hard and needed money.

Looking at the coffee table Troy noticed the unpaid utility bill. He pointed at it and asked, "Do you mind if I open this up and take a look at it?"

"Why sure you can," answered Chester. "It's just a bill we can't afford to pay."

Troy picked up the bill and opened it. It represented a final notice for a three month past due account. Their electricity would soon be turned off if the delinquency continued. He reached into his pocket and pulled out his cell phone and wallet. He called the phone number on the bill and said, "I'd like to pay off a bill."

The room remained silent. The couple tensed up with hope that they would not lose their power. Troy was transferred to the billing department. Using the information on the statement he identified the house by an account number and used the name Chester Carlton. Troy got out his debit card and used the numbers on it to liquidate the power bill. It was all taken care of with the Carltons being guaranteed that they would survive another winter.

This act of humanity compelled Ben to contribute even further. He pulled out his wallet and gave them the remaining twenty dollars that he borrowed from Troy a week ago, leaving just one dollar left. Handing it to the man of the house Ben said, "I want you to have this."

Chester took the money with dignity. He looked at Troy and Ben and said, "We would not have survived if it wasn't for you. I just wish that we could do something in return."

"All we want is to know if there is anything else we can do for you," replied Ben.

Troy nodded his head in agreement. He then realized that he was overdue to check up on his mother. Troy stood up and said, "I need to go now. It was wonderful to see you two today. Please keep in touch and always let us know if you need anything."

On that note, Troy stood up with Ben and shook hands with the feeble couple. Farewells were exchanged with Troy and Ben walking to the front door and leaving the refurbished house. Once outside Troy said, "I admire what you did for them."

"I'm just trying to keep up with you," Ben countered. Ben looked at his watch and saw that it was almost three o'clock. He was beat, hungry, and down to his last dollar. Still, he was at peace with himself knowing that he did the *right thing*.

Troy offered him a ride home. "No, thanks," said Ben. "I don't live far from here and I like a good walk. See you at the hall tonight."

"I'll be looking for you," said Troy as he patted his friend on the back.

Ben always viewed winter as a gift from nature. He could now admire the beauty of crystallized snow under radiant sunshine. The blue sky also reminded him of how fortunate they were. Clear weather enabled them to work outside despite the cold. Most importantly, he was made aware of the Carlton's plight. He saw that they were worse off than he was. The family man could now place them under his wing by praying and keeping a close eye.

It was a good day for Ben Skates.

Chapter V

ARRIVING HOME, BEN NOTICED that his red pickup truck was gone. He remembered Gloria making a comment that morning asking him if he needed anything specific from the store. He entered his home and went straight to the utility room, throwing his soiled work clothes into the washing machine. Immediately, he went upstairs to the master bedroom and took a shower. After drying off, the tried man crawled into bed and took a nap.

Ben woke up to the irresistible smell of Gloria's cooking. He dressed and went downstairs into the dining room. He saw a table setting for only three and remembered that Sam had plans with his friends that night.

He realized that soon his boy would be off to college. At that moment something else dawned on him. Susan was not far behind her brother and would eventually be out in the world herself.

He took his position by extending open hands. A human circle was formed with heads bowing in gratitude. Once again, the ceremony of grace took place in the Skates household.

It was now time for the famished man to enjoy warm leftovers with the company of his wife and daughter. Ben would first gaze at the beautiful mother and daughter team that sat before him. He addressed his little girl first. "Susan," said the father. "Tell us how the modeling seminar went today."

The fifteen year old's eyes bulged with excitement. It was apparent that she had a lot to report. Looking back and forth at her parents she started to talk. "It was wonderful," she exclaimed. She picked up a glass of milk and took a big drink. Placing it down she started to go into detail. Ben took a hefty bite of meatloaf as he gave full attention to Susan. The hardy meatloaf seemed to taste even better the second time around.

The high school sophomore's description of the seminar sounded more like a convention. Wide-eyed she addressed both parents by saying, "Every modeling agency in the region had representatives there!" Ben looked at Gloria and saw how proud she was. Susan went on to tell how nice the representatives were and how they all offered assistance.

Then came a somber moment. Susan's voice started to get choppy as she leaned towards her father. Her shoulders tensed as she lowered her head. Innocent brown eyes rolled up to look at the man of the house. "Dad," she said in a soft trembling voice.

"What is it?" he asked.

A nervous Susan continued as her eyes bounced around the table. "Last month I told you that I need to have a portfolio made with glamor shots. I know that it's expensive, but..."

Ben interrupted as he pulled his wallet out of his back pocket. The conscientious father never forgot about his daughter's request. He calculated what it would take to earn the money that would come out of his dwindling savings account. He believed that when school let out for the summer and work picked up, he would then be able to replace the money. A check was removed from his wallet and placed on the table between the mother and daughter.

Together the women leaned against each other and looked down at it. Slowly their faces went from a blank stare to an ear to ear grin that only a winning game show contestant could display. What was supposed to be one-hundred and thirty dollars was two hundred. They looked up at Ben with their jaws dropped.

"I figured that you two are overdue to have a day together," he said. "There should be enough there to buy Susan a new outfit for the pictures and then you two can also have lunch somewhere."

Susan broke into tears of relief as she got up and ran to her father. Her arms wrapped around the best father in town as she said, "Thank you, dad. I love you so much..."

Gloria joined in. "I have to get in on this too!" she proclaimed. Leaving her chair, she raced to her husband and hugged his head, kissing the top of it over and over again. The big man's arms embraced the girls into one big emotional group hug that lasted minutes.

Dinner was eventually resumed with a happy Susan eating the delicious meal while glancing back and forth at her parents. Once the meal was finished, Susan insisted that she clear the table and wash the dishes.

"I don't have a problem with that," commented the father with a slight laugh. At that moment a faint knock could be heard at the front door. Looking up at the clock on the dining room wall he safely assumed who it would be. A glance at Gloria turned into a nod that signaled she would start a pot of tea.

Like most people, Sharon Wilson was a creature of habit. She never asked for anything two days in a row. Instead she always returned the following day with a small token of appreciation, like the cookies he received that morning.

Ben opened the door to see blue eyes looking up at him. It was no surprise to see that the visitor also held a gift: more chocolate chip cookies. "Please come in, Mrs. Wilson," greeted Ben with a neighborly jest.

There was ample time to visit with the frail senior. It would last until Ben had to go to the fellowship hall. This would serve as a 'trump card' to walk her home. For the time-being, they would share tea and listen to a recap of Mrs. Wilson's day in front a cozy fire.

Two hours later Ben was on his own walking past his old high school. He eventually crossed the crest of the hill that opened up to the heart of town. Being Friday night there was some activity around and about. The bowling alley seemed to be the hot spot with a coffee shop and two cafes batting cleanup. Ben set his sights further down towards the freeway ramp.

And there it was...

A scout from the fellowship hall dressed in full costume holding a sign. Most of the town wasn't even aware of the lonesome figure that blended in with the darkness. Ben walked on the opposite side of the street as he approached the hall. He gave a slight motion to acknowledge his teammate while trying to be inconspicuous in public. The shivering hobo gave a slight wave in return.

Ben entered the hall and saw that it was almost a full house. Scanning the room he noticed Troy and Gene motioning him to come over. Ben waved at them and pointed at the coffee stand; they understood that he would get a cup of coffee on his way to the table. Once seated, Gene spoke up. "I was just talking about what you asked us the other night," he said. "About if our families were aware of us holding a sign out there in that outfit."

Ben wanted to hear more. "And?" he questioned.

Gene continued. "If they suspected, I think that they would have asked at least one of us by now. Nobody here has been asked that question yet."

Troy leaned back in his chair and nodded in agreement. "I think that we've done a good job hiding this thing so far," Gene added.

"I hope you're right," said Ben.

Ben was startled by a tapping on his shoulder. He turned around and saw Jake West standing over him. Jake was the father of Ryan West, a classmate of his son. Ryan was also a promising outfielder on the team and a distant candidate for a scholarship. His career was greatly overshadowed by the many records Sam broke. The boys palled around like 'Fric and Frak' with Ryan playing second fiddle.

This frustrated Jake to no end. *His* high school career was everything to him but was overshadowed by a legendary teammate who also set records: Ben Skates.

Jake still wore his high school letterman's sweater around town; it suggested a subliminal way to cry foul over recognition he felt was denied. Being almost five inches shorter didn't help his esteem any.

"Did you hear the news?" asked Jake.

"What news?" asked Ben.

The partially bald man with a goatee and slicked back black hair raised his voice loud enough for the entire room to hear. "It looks like my boy will be playing baseball for state next year," he announced puffing out his chest. Putting his hand on Ben's muscular shoulder Jake spoke to him in a condescending tone. "I wouldn't be too concerned; I think that your boy will make it too."

Ben had nothing to prove. He was the bigger man and responded in an adult-like fashion. "I appreciate that," he said in a smooth, calm voice.

Ben did himself a favor by addressing topics more important to him. Looking at Troy he asked, "How is your mother?"

Troy slid back and gritted his teeth to hold in the laughter. He started to tell a story about how she worries about him if he's gone for over an hour. The sweet story about his mother's unconditional love cleared out the bad vibes he was getting from his high school rival.

After a few more accounts of his mother's actions it was Gene's turn.

Gene Fletcher was a bear of a man. In high school he was the all-state lineman who physically pushed defenders around to create holes for the running game. He played local college ball and stayed home to raise a family in the very small town atmosphere he had growing up. The part-time trucker was also a mechanic at several jobs that Ben worked at. The 42-year-old man was devoted to his pretty wife Dora. He also lived for his 9-year-old daughter, Grace and 7-year-old daughter, Angelia.

He commented on how his wife and daughters always do projects together. "Sometimes they find a real good hiding place in our home and secretly make me a gift they spent weeks on," he said in a bewildered tone. "Lately they have been acting strange," he continued. "They got an old Easter basket and started to dress it up with bows and ribbons. They're putting all sorts of goodies into it too: canned salmon, crackers, cheeses, nuts, olives, and lots and lots of candy. The part that gets me is that they are not hiding this from me. They kept this project on our family room table in plain sight."

The handsome African American in the blue coveralls started to laugh at himself as he used his hands to express further. "They even work on it right in front of me but won't tell me who it's for. They only say that it's for someone who is loved by God. Whoever this special person is will definitely love this gift. They're even making a homemade card with their handprints all over it."

Troy and Ben listened to every word Gene said. They knew his family and were aware how charitable they were.

Troy commented first, "Wow..."

Ben followed, "Wow..."

An unexpected cold breeze came rushing into the room as the front door opened. A transient-looking figure holding a cardboard sign entered and quickly closed the door. The masked man walked up to the podium and dropped a few coins into the brass urn. Next he dropped in a few wrinkled dollars.

The masked marvel turned to his audience. All at once he took off the hat and mask to reveal his true identity. It was Glenn Holmes, a respected employee at the local grocery store. The heavy-set 45-year-old raised his hands in victory. "Four dollars and sixty-one cents!" exclaimed the single father with bushy blonde hair. He immediately began to dance around in circles as everyone stood up and applauded. Glenn was that man in the grocery store who always made others happy. He was a special member in the hall who always lifted everyone's spirits.

"Well, I guess it's my turn," said Gene. He got up and sat down next to Glenn in front of the portable heater. They began to undress and dress as they bantered back and forth with a few chuckles in between. Soon Glenn was stretched out in front of the heater with a hot cup of soup in hand. "Good luck out there," he said to Gene as his replacement walked to the door.

Gene waved a hand over his head to let the hall know he was ready for his shift. The former football player left the building to do *his* rendition of 'Elmo.'

Some nights Elmo appeared to be a little taller. On others he seemed more stout. These subtle changes were obscured by the shadows of the night and relatively unnoticeable to the naked eye. The hobo outfit barely fit the large man, but it still made the sell. Gene Fletcher stopped at the corner of Elm Street and Main, cautiously looking both ways. The intersection was clear and he crossed the street. As he approached the curve he noticed the reflections of many shiny objects scattered about. Someone who cared threw what spare change they had at the isolated corner with size thirteen footprints. This gave Gene a warm feeling inside as he scavenged for the scraps of charity. *Goodness gracious*, thought Gene. *Whoever did this must have emptied their entire piggy bank..."*

A childhood fantasy came to mind.

As a boy, Gene always loved Easter and Halloween. He imagined the fun he and his friends would have with a night time Easter egg hunt. This called for eggs that were made of gold and glowed in the dark. He suddenly stopped with a revelation.

Looking up to the moon lit winter night with glistening stars he realized that God had arranged such an Easter egg hunt. The child came out in him as he delicately looked for more gold on the silver ground.

More Heavenly gifts were on their way.

A set of headlights honed in on the child at play. It came from a recognizable blue minivan that parked directly in front of him with its doors opening. Leaving the vehicle was a beautiful African American woman holding a tall decorated Easter basket full of treats with a card sticking out of the top. She was accompanied by two young girls. Together, they all wore matching pink and white wintertime outfits that signified they were family.

They walked towards the panhandler and stopped within six feet. The threesome huddled with the mother giving instructions. The daughters extended their arms as the basket was handed to them. Each girl grabbed hold of the handle and turned around. The mother along with her two children marched up to the silent hobo and gave a presentation.

The eldest child spoke first. "We want to give this to you because God loves you."

The younger child continued. "We baked cookies and made a card for you too."

The mother joined in. "This is a good town with many good people struggling to survive. You will always be in our prayers and I know that things will get better for you soon."

Watery brown eyes were covered by the tilted hat. The enormous body started to shake as a gloved hand reached out to accept the basket. Feeling the weight of the handle, he retrieved it with both hands. Looking down at his midnight Easter basket, the grown man started to sob. The man in the hobo outfit avoided eye contact and remained silent. An exaggerated nodding of his head was the only way the mime could express gratitude.

The mother knew that the man needed to be alone now. She corralled her daughters and walked them back to the van.

They turned and waved goodbye with Gene waving back. "We love you," was the final message sent as they entered the warm vehicle and drove away.

The mighty man just had a childhood dream fulfilled by current standards. This left him an emotional wreck with barely enough strength to walk back to the hall.

Troy and Ben were discussing their day with the Carltons when Gene entered the room. They knew something had to be wrong for him to return within an hour. The strong man entered the room holding the basket and sign, placing them on an empty table closest to the door. He proceeded to the brass urn and emptied both pockets. Next he took off the suit in front of the portable heater and left it on the floor. Wearing only a red jogging outfit in stocking feet he walked to the furthest corner of the room to isolate himself. The big man rested his face on the table in front of him with his arms resting on either side. All eyes were on him as he began to cry like a child.

Gene was honored and left alone. Those present turned to the lone table by the door and saw the basket next to the sign. The festive bows and ribbons outlined the variety of treats it held. The basket resembled a Christmas tree with the card serving as the traditional star on top. It was beautiful all in its own, offering encouragement and goodwill to anyone who saw it.

Chapter VI

SATURDAY ARRIVED WITH ALL its glory. Ben woke up to the flavorful smell of hickory smoked bacon. Taking a deep breath he detected the aroma of rich coffee harmonized with it. "This is going to be a good breakfast," he said to himself. Ben threw off the covers and got dressed. Running out of the bedroom and down the stairs he yelled, "Don't start without me!"

Ben continued down the hallway that led into the kitchen. Once inside he saw that his family had their backs turned. To the right was a teenage girl with her hair pinned up wearing pink pajamas outlined with red hearts. In the middle was a grown woman with her hair pinned up wearing white pants with a blue sweater. To the left was an athletic 17-year-old wearing jeans and a baseball jersey.

The middle person moved first slightly with all three turning around at the same time. What Ben saw was hysterical. Each was holding a strip of bacon in their mouth with an innocent expression. "Did you say something, my dear?" asked Gloria in a sophisticated tone.

The poker faces lost their composure and bent over laughing. Ben fanned the coals by responding in a childish tone, "But, what about me?"

"Well, what about you?" fired back Susan.

Gloria got down to business. "How many pancakes do you want?"

Ben looked surprised and questioned, "Pancakes?"

"Yes, pancakes," she answered.

"Put a great-big stack on the table and then we'll go from there," he heartily suggested rubbing his hands together.

Gloria reached behind her and said, "And you'll be needing this..." She had his favorite cup full of coffee and handed to him, kissing him on his cheek.

Saturday mornings were always special. The family was now sitting down saying grace. The platter of hotcakes made its way around the table with Ben getting the remaining four. Butter followed with maple syrup close behind. Bacon was plentiful with six strips reaching Ben's plate. The family knew that this was dad's favorite breakfast.

Ben took a four layer bite of the maple flavored pancakes and slowly chewed with his eyes closed. He swallowed the first bite and opened his eyes. "Does anyone have any plans today?" he asked.

Gloria had an answer. "Well it just so happens that we do," she said gazing at Susan. "There was a nice man that gave us enough money to get Susan's hair done and buy her a new outfit."

Susan stared at her dad with loving eyes.

Ben was happy to see the mother and daughter bonding that took place on a regular basis. It was something very special—just between the two of them. It was just like the same bond he had with his son. Looking at Sam he remembered all the times they went to the playing field he used to pitch at, the times he taught him how to throw a hardball, and the many talks they had in the empty bleachers about *baseball teaching life*.

"Well," said the father as he looked at his son. "I guess that it's just me and you today."

Sam gave his reply. "Well, not exactly," he said as he picked up a piece of bacon and bit into it.

Ben was hurt. He could see that his son was growing up and slowly distancing himself from the man who shared his dreams. Sam would have the last laugh though. He was not just a good baseball player; he was also excellent on the school plays he performed in.

Looking across the table at his dad, Sam finished what he had to say. "Do you remember the baseball scouts that looked at us after school this week?"

Ben answered cautiously, "Yes I do." He raised one eyebrow and wanted to hear more.

Sam continued. "They are going to my school today to get a further look at some of us. Coach Jenkins will open up the school to let them in."

Ben felt like he was slowly becoming a has been in his son's life. He did his best not to show the pain. "Well, good," he said. "You have a good time and show em' your stuff."

"Dad," said Sam with direct eye contact. "They want to see where my arm came from. You have to go with me."

Ben was relieved. He was still 'one of the guys.' "I'll be there," promised the former stand-out as he winked at his son.

Breakfast continued with each parent planning the day's events with their assigned partner. Once the last slice of bacon swiped a remaining trace of maple syrup, Sam and Susan cleared the table and cleaned the kitchen. This gave Ben a moment to kiss his wife and thank her for a great breakfast. But there was more than that; he thanked her for everything.

The guys left first with Sam dressed in his uniform. With glove in hand, they went outside and began their walk. It was now 'father and son' time.

"Son," addressed the dad in a serious tone. "Can you take some advice from a guy that's been around?"

Sam stopped and made a statement to his father. "Dad, I need you now more than ever."

The father looked at his son 'man-to-man.' Speaking in a tone of authority he gave his advice. "When you are around those scouts, don't say a thing."

Sam starred back closed mouthed and nodded with the understanding.

"They already know what you are as a high school player," explained the former pitching star. "Now they're sizing you up as a man. Just do what they ask of you and be in control by not being nervous. Only speak when spoken to and be as brief as possible about it... and that's it."

Pride beamed through his son's eyes as he professionally remained quiet. They continued their walk and approached Sharon Wilson's house. The frequent guest waved through her view window as the men waved back.

Within minutes they were on campus with a few cars in the parking lot. The door closest to the baseball field was propped opened. Ben and Sam entered and walked down the hallway that displayed the athletic highlights throughout the school's history. The first few documentations included Sam's illustrious career. The dad put his arm around his son, clenched his right hand and affectionately rubbed it into his cheek. Each step went further back in time until Ben's era came into view. Several more newspaper articles were framed with the name Skates littered in bold print. Sam elbowed his father as they pretended not to notice. The end of the hall was decorated by framed yellowed newsprint that frequently had the name Skates in bold print.

The gymnasium was a few feet away. Just before entering, a familiar voice could be heard. Ben and Sam looked at each other with Sam's eyes rolling around telegraphing confusion. The father communicated back by looking down at his feet. He illustrated embarrassment by shaking his head with his eyes closed.

They entered the gym to see Jake West entertaining the college scouts.

The father in the letterman's sweater was doing his best to hold his own, telling stories of his baseball career and relating it to his son. Ryan stood back quietly and listened. The scouts were not on the time clock yet and could afford to be cordial.

The moment reminded Ben of a topic that once took place in the local barbershop. Those present debated how good Jake would do selling used cars.

Sam was noticed by a tall man in a black three piece suit sporting a red tie. He had distinct short white hair and was definitely one of the many scouts that evaluated him recently. He politely left during the middle of a story and made a beeline to Sam.

As he approached a popular State University tie clip became visible. He smiled at Sam but addressed his father first. "Are you Ben Skates?" he asked.

Ben stood proud. "Yes I am," he replied extending his hand.

"Phil Downs," replied the man as they shook hands. Phil was personable and made a humorous comment. Pointing at Sam he said, "So this is the guy that broke the records from the guy that broke his grandfather's records."

That statement let Ben and Sam know that this scout knew *everything* about the Skate legacy. Sam remained quiet.

Phil had more to say. "I feel that I have seen enough of your son's ability. He will, however, be reviewed a little further today by some of our position coaches. If they like what they see I hope that I personally get to give your entire family a tour of our university."

"We would appreciate that," said Ben with firmness. Phil Shook hands with Ben and motioned to shake Sam's.

"I am very impressed with you Sam," he said while shaking his hand. "Put on a good show today."

"I will do my very best today, Mr. Downs," said Sam with a tone of confidence. "Thank you for being here."

"It's my pleasure," replied Phil Downs. He swiftly turned around and exited the gym.

Ben looked at his son and said, "You were perfect."

Coach Jenkins blew his whistle and called out a name. "Sam Skates, you are needed up here at once." The dad looked at his son and said nothing. He bumped him with his shoulder as he walked to the bleachers. Ben started to climb the incline until he was almost at the top. Sam walked to his coach with his glove already on.

Ben watched his son receive instructions from Coach Jenkins. At that moment, the father who thought he was sitting alone was startled. "Is that your son?" asked a strange voice.

Ben looked to his left and saw a man wearing a jean jacket with matching pants. He was somewhat medium in stature and had black hair with a crew cut. The tanned face with dark rimmed prescription glasses did not match this part of the country.

There was something about him that made Ben think he might have seen him before. He had to question himself. Maybe he briefly noticed him at the store or in the bank. He could possibly have been a new face at the fellowship hall that he forgot to introduce himself to.

"Yes he is," answered Ben.

Sam got up to the makeshift mound on the basketball court and began to warm up.

"Hey," said the man with intense black eyes. "He looks pretty good."

"Thanks," he replied. It was time to be introduced. "My name is Ben," he said as he leaned over extending his hand.

"I'm Stanley," countered the visitor as their hands met.

Sam was done warming up and nodded his head to his coach. The baseball scouts positioned themselves where everyone had a good vantage point. A cardboard cutout of a batter was placed inside the batter's box. The fully dressed catcher got out of his stance and trotted up to Sam. They had a brief conference ending with Sam nodding his head. The catcher trotted back behind the plate and relayed the signals that the coach was signaling to him.

It was showtime.

Sam concentrated on his mark and did his wind-up. With determination he threw the ball as a 'pop' sound echoed off the catcher's glove. The catcher tossed the ball back to Sam as he established a pitching rhythm.

With the grace of Sugar Ray Leonard and the finesse of Wayne Gretzky, his pitches grew sharper and sharper. Stanley looked at Ben in awe and commented, "He's the best I've ever seen!"

Ben commented back in a soft voice. "He's the best I've ever seen..."

The exhibition lasted for twenty minutes with the cutout being repositioned, but never hit. Once done, all stood in an ovation. Sam was surrounded by his coach and the scouts. Ben knew his place and remained distant.

Stanley addressed Ben. "That was sensational," he said. "You must be proud of him."

Ben was beginning to feel more comfortable around Stanley. Leaning back he said, "Thank you, and I am."

Stanley asked Ben a question. "Do you have a minute?"

"Sure I do," he said.

"What's it like to live here?" asked Stanley.

Ben leaned back and looked towards the ceiling as he tried to find the right words. "Well," he said, "the citizens here are wonderful from the youngest child to the oldest person. Our problem is that we share the same problem that the rest of the country is having; our economy has taken a bad hit." Ben's sincere brown eyes looked at Stanley. "Other than that, this is a great place to raise a family."

Stanley seemed to interrogate. "Are you working?"

Ben turned towards him and leaned forward, resting his hands on his lap. "If you call twenty hours a week to support a family of four working, then you can say that I am."

"It must be tough," said Stanley.

"It is," said Ben. "You are talking to a man who only has one dollar in his wallet."

Stanley dark eyes stared at Ben's with penetration. "Would you give that dollar to a man who is far from home and looking for a place to stay?" he asked.

Ben looked at him and detected something awkward. *What's wrong with this picture?* He couldn't put his finger on it though. Ben began to question. "Are you that man far from home and looking for shelter?"

Stanley was strong and remained focused. "Yes I am," he said.

Ben reached into his back pocket and pulled out his wallet. He took out his last dollar and handed it to Stanley. "I guess you need this more than I do," he said in a gentleman type voice. Stanley reached for the dollar and took it out of his hand.

Ben didn't stop there. He told Stanley about the fellowship hall off of Elm Street. "You will always have a place to go and get as much soup as you want. You can even stay there; we have bunks in the back room."

What Ben said registered with Stanley. "I'll remember that," he said. "Thanks for the dollar." The strange man put the bill in the front pocket of his jean jacket and asked one last question. "What happens if the hall is closed and it's freezing outside?"

Ben had an answer. With conviction he stared back and calmly said. "Then you'll just have to come to my home and stay with us." Ben leaned closer to him and whispered, "Nobody in this town will ever starve or be homeless."

Stanley continued to stare at Ben as he digested the information.

Ben looked away and saw his son standing in front of the bleachers. The successful pitcher got his dad's attention and displayed a big thumbs up. Ben extended his arm and returned the gesture.

"It was a pleasure meeting you, Stanley," said Ben as he extended his hand one last time.

"I appreciated meeting you," said Stanley as he clasped Ben's hand and shook in farewell.

Ben stood up and walked down to his son. "You looked good son," said the proud father as he put his arm around the prodigy.

"Thanks, dad," replied Sam.

The father and son team left for home. It was still Saturday and Ben wanted to spend the rest of the day with his friends. "Sure you can," authorized his father.

"Dad," asked Ben, "can you give me a twenty so that I can eat out with my friends tonight?"

That request killed Ben. He was out of money until the following week unless he withdrew what little he had left in savings, or borrowed more off of Troy.

"I'd like to, but at this moment I don't have anything on me," explained the father.

"That's okay dad," said Sam with an upbeat attitude. "There's no need for you to knock yourself out. I have bought for my friends before and I know that one of them will cover me."

Ben was relieved. He was being honest with his son without 'tipping his hand.' Still, he momentarily felt like a failure. *A dad should always have a little spending money for his son's outings,* thought Ben.

The day would finish out with the girls in town, Sam being with his friends, and dad eventually moonlighting by the freeway ramp.

Chapter VII

BEN WENT SOLO FOR the rest of the afternoon. He did a few mundane chores around the house but got bored and left for the hall earlier than usual. He would arrive before sunset with 'Elmo' not deployed yet.

For the second time that day he encountered a loud, noxious voice. In fact, it was the same voice he heard in the gymnasium that morning. Entering the fellowship hall he spotted Jake West captivating his audience with another story. This one was about his reenactment on what happened earlier that day. "You should have seen the looks on their faces when they watched my boy!" he boasted.

The town of Miner was a small town where news traveled fast. Heads turned when Ben entered the room. Silent gestures followed that told the word was already out about his son's performance. After all, the Skates name was always known for representing the town well. Ben quietly nodded and took a seat. Jake continued telling his story.

A surprise visitor entered the room with a grand entrance that needed no introduction. It was Pete Rainwater, a popular Native

American that cared about the community. "Howdy, howdy, howdy," greeted the 57-year-old.

The rugged man seemed to come out of the prairie from a hundred years ago. A dark Stetson hat covered strong cheekbones with piercing black eyes. His buckskin vest, Levis, and cowboy boots displayed his proud heritage.

There was more to the man than his dynamic presence. He was a role model who raised his three children before taking to the woods. On occasion he would drop by the fellowship hall to visit, but never gossip. This was because he had an uncanny knack for knowing the town's latest news before it spread. The contented bachelor loved to participate in anything that helped the community. He looked over at Ben and with a mere glance, praised his son. Ben smiled back with appreciation.

Pete arrived carrying a steaming pot of his renowned stew. It was a homemade concoction that spawned from his livelihood of gardening and hunting. With class, he placed it on the kitchen counter with the chicken noodle soup and coffee. The humanitarian returned and sat down amongst friends.

The sun had just set, creating the protection of nightfall. It was also Saturday night; the night where the freeway ramp would yield its highest bounty. "I better get out there," said Troy Meeker.

"I believe it's my turn," said Pete. "Besides, you have some stew to eat," he added.

Ben spoke up. "Pete, you have already done so much for this town and have never leaned on this hall in any way."

Pete responded. "This is all about having families survive, so count me in." He followed protocol by sitting in front of the portable heater, stripping down to his gray sweat outfit, and putting on the hobo costume piece by piece.

Once done, he stood up and addressed the room. "Should I wear this during the summer when the carnival comes to town so that I can sell balloons?" Laughter thundered throughout the room as Pete walked to the door, picked up the sign, and went to his post.

Pete actually enjoyed being alone outside, but tonight it would be short-lived. He peacefully studied the surrounding hills that was once home for his ancestors and prayed to their souls. Suddenly, he encountered a strange feeling; he could sense that something *wrong* was coming his way.

Faint music could be heard in the distance and grew louder with every second. A set of headlights could now be seen approaching him as the noise increased. He saw the fast moving vehicle bounce on the icy road and assumed the passengers must be mischievous teenagers out on a joyride.

He wasn't far from the truth.

The vehicle was a rusted brown pickup truck with several boys in the back. It slid to a stop in front of Pete with a loud voice singing out, "Hey, Elbowroom, get a job!"

The men in the hall heard the loud radio playing from the vehicle outside and the calling for 'Elmo.' They looked at each other and suddenly realized that Pete was in trouble. The delayed reaction only allowed them enough time to watch from the hall's front door.

Pete met a batter's worst fear; he saw Sam Skates standing tall and winding up to throw. Instinctively, Pete turned sideways and began to take cover. Sam wind milled a white deteriorating blur that disintegrated upon hitting his left shoulder. The fragments of the snowball sprayed his upper body. Pete recovered and recognized Ryan West in form. He quickly pirouetted as his opposite shoulder was struck. Two more snowballs hit Pete then the truck sped off into the night.

It was all over within seconds.

Pete saw his support run over to his aid. The men asked Pete if he was okay. "I'm fine," he assured. They walked him back to the fellowship hall to double check if he was injured.

He took off the hat and mask and looked at Ben. "That boy of yours certainly has a great arm!" he reported with excitement. "It traveled so fast that I couldn't see it coming." Pete turned sideways and showed where the snowball hit. "He should make it in the majors easy," predicted Pete as he nodded his head with approval.

Ben was too ashamed of what his son did and couldn't speak.

Once again, Jake West felt a distant second. "What about my boy's arm?" he asked.

Pete said, "It's not bad." He turned around and showed the mark Ryan left on his other shoulder. Jake got within inches of the imprint and beamed with pride.

"I will finish up out there tonight," said Ben. "It's the least I can do." He sat down next to Pete and stripped down to his long johns, eventually becoming Elmo. Without saying a word he left with sign in hand.

The atmosphere was more jubilant down the street at Ella's Coffee Shop. A rusty brown pickup truck was parked in back with five boys sharing a booth.

"Are you sure you don't mind covering me?" asked Sam Skates.

"Sam," replied Paul Muller. "You have bought for all of us at one time or another; let me get this." Paul was honored to have a friendship with Sam. He was only a freshman and got to hang out with Sam and Ryan, the two most popular guys in school. The skinny kid with red hair and freckles achieved status at a young age.

"Thanks," said Sam.

The topic changed into one of celebration.

"Sam, that was great how you creamed Elmo!" exclaimed Tim Wesson. Tim was a baseball player who started for the junior varsity squad. He always sat as close as he could to Sam whenever possible. He knew of the Skate's legacy and wanted to be viewed as Sam's future replacement. He even had brown hair with matching eyes that suggested being related. Tim even combed his hair like Sam did, unbeknownst to him. A letterman's jacket with a baseball jersey made him appear as a younger brother. Tim always laughed at every joke his idol told.

There was another selling point that also came with Tim. He was the only one in the clique that had a car.

"Hey, didn't I register a good hit?" asked Ryan West.

"You did good," said Tim. "But Sam's almost knocked him over."

Ella Ray was the proprietor of the coffee shop that doubled as a malt shop. The woman was clearing tables and couldn't help but hear the conversation. She was home grown and knew the community. The business owner was in her playful seventies and a former classmate of Sam's grandfather, Will Skates. Like all the girls her age, she too had an incurable crush on him. Her daughter was equally drawn to Ben Skates, an attraction that started way back in grade school. Ella's granddaughter had an eye for Sam.

Wild gray hair captured the freedom of the blue-eyed woman in the wire rim glasses. Sometimes a tie-dyed shirt would surface as the former *hippie chick* went through life without a care.

Ella was no fool though. She was streetwise and very perceptive. The classy lady was also personable and respected. She was the right person to run a place where teenagers could hang out.

Ella walked up to the table to take the order. "How's your evening going?" she asked the familiar faces.

"Better than someone else we know of," laughed Paul. The five boys bent over in hysterics.

Ella looked sideways at the table. "Well...it sounds funny," she said. "Are you going to let me in on it?"

"We paid a dear old friend a visit tonight and gave him a gift," said Ryan cleverly.

Ella sensed something out of place. "Who was the friend?" she asked with a sincere look.

"Elmo," answered Jeff Turner as he held both hands against his stomach, busting out with laughter. The whole table leaned forward shaking in tears. Jeff was a different breed that wasn't athletic but added something extra to the group. The lean boy with black wavy hair had a part time job after school and was fascinated with computers. He was intelligent and usually very responsible.

"Elmo?" she questioned. "Who's Elmo?"

"That bum down the street that refuses to work," said an agitated Sam Skates.

Ella looked away with a blank expression as she tried to piece the puzzle together. A horrified look came over her face as she turned around. The elder pulled out a nearby chair that was facing her. She straddled the seat while holding onto the back rest. "Do you mean that homeless man that comes out at night by the freeway?" she asked.

"That's the one," said Paul.

"Did you hurt that man?" she asked.

"Not really," said Tim. "We just let him know that it was time for him to get a job, that's all."

Ella's knuckles began to turn white. "What did you do to him?" she asked.

"We only threw snowballs and told him to get a job," said Ryan.

Ella's jaw dropped from disappointment and wasted no time addressing the lead dog. She gathered her composure and focused on Sam. Leaning inches away from his face she spoke in a polite tone. "Can I talk to you for a minute in the kitchen?" she asked.

Sam squirmed like a student being reprimanded in class. He knew that his friends took great pleasure watching how uncomfortable he was and would rib him about it for months. Ella walked to the kitchen. Sam looked at the shaking, tense faces that fought back laughter. He slid out of the booth and marched to the kitchen to face the music.

Once inside, he saw Ella sitting at a card table. She pointed at an empty chair facing her that was pulled out for him. He knew the scenario. The tough woman was utilizing the same approach his father used. He sat down and scooted the chair to the table. Ben knew the ground rules: at all times there must be eye-contact without any interruptions.

The first round would be the traditional silence needed to level the playing field, with Ella starring directly at him. Once accomplished, the cagy woman would fire the first salvo.

What seemed like an eternity was only a few intense seconds with Ella moving forward. "Do you know what the name Skates means to this town?" she asked in a controlling voice.

Sam knew his place and followed the advice his father gave him for the college scouts. He remained motionless and quiet.

Ella continued. "It's the most respected name we will ever know," she said. "Your family is the backbone that made this town."

Ben gave a micro-second quiver as if an ice cube was dropped down his back. He continued to listen while holding his hands on the table.

"Your grandfather attended my high school when I was there," Ella said. "He carried the same respect your father did."

Sam took a dry swallow and began to fight tears.

Leaning closer the woman extended both her hands to hold Sam's. Maintaining her sincere look she said something that the boy was not aware of. "Do you realize that everyone in Miner looks up to you with the same respect?"

That comment gave Sam a jolt. He was not expecting any compliments and sat up wanting to hear more.

Ella stayed on course. "Your grandfather, Will, was the man of our class," she said. "He represented all of us by wearing our school uniform when he played baseball." The youthful senior let go of his hands as she looked up to the ceiling. Her face contorted with joy as she went back in time. "He was the state's best baseball player and people traveled for miles to watch him play," she recalled.

Sam listened in awe with a blank expression.

"When he stood on that mound we all looked at him as if he was our own father," she said. Looking at Sam she gave a brief laugh adding, "But there were those of us that imagined being married to him one day."

Sam nodded back with a smile.

With her arms wrapped around her head she looked up and covered more detail. "He received national recognition for winning a championship for the smallest town in the state. His feat put this town on the map and everyone knew who we were," said Ella as she playfully swayed back and forth. "He had a presence on that mound that was dignified. But there was so much more to him than being our star pitcher."

At that moment she put her arms on the table and sat up looking at Sam. "He was a good man that cared for everybody," she proclaimed. "Will was still humble even though he could have had any girl he wanted. He was respected because he showed respect. Every student in school knew him as a friend who always put others first."

Sam let the information sink in.

"He was like your father," pointed out Ella. "My daughter and I would watch your dad play on the same field he did. I could see the similarities between the two and shared them with my daughter. They had the same class, same dignity, and carried an equal amount of respect. We would compare stories about our high school years having a Skates in our class. That's what every parent in this town wanted, to have their child be classmates with someone from your family."

Sam was taken by her words and slid back in his chair.

Ella had more to say. "Your dad was written up in the papers many times," she said. "He even won a championship for us, just like you did."

Ella was hitting home with the boy.

"That's not why this town looks up to your family, though," she expressed. "Skates aren't viewed as great baseball players who

Elmo

are great men; they are known as great men who are also great baseball players."

Sam froze like a statue, absorbing the tidbit.

Parenting skills now came out of Ella. "Why do you think those boys out there hang out with you?" she questioned eventually giving the answer. "It's because they want your image."

Sam looked off to the side realizing that she was right.

Ella had more. "They act completely different when they're here without you," she confided. "Tonight, they did things differently; they got you to be like them."

Sam tensed up and turned beet red. It dawned on him what really happened that night. He slowly looked up with the foolish expression of a child caught in a lie.

Ella would now drive in the final stake. "Now about Elmo," she said. "Is he possibly someone out there who knew that the Skates family lived in this town?"

That triggered Sam. He sat up straight and knew what to do. "I have to go now," he said looking at her. "Thank you."

"You are very welcome," she said. "I have faith in you, Sam,"

Sam Skates got up and left the kitchen with his *friends* anxiously waiting for him. He quickly walked up to the booth, picked up his jacket and started to leave.

It occurred to Ryan that he was now top seed. He yelled out, "What's the matter, are you going to kiss Elmo?" Sam didn't have to prove himself. He simply walked out the door without saying a word. The other boys remained quiet.

71

Sam was on a mission to put *right* what was *wronged*. This would however, require breaking a few eggs to make the omelet. On more than one occasion his father reminded him that at night he had boundaries. One of which being the last stretch on Main Street that led to the freeway ramp. "It's poorly lit with cars and trucks driving too fast," would be his reasoning. There was a bit more to it than that, but Ben justified leaving some things out. Until that evening, Sam never challenged his jurisdiction.

Sam couldn't forgive himself until he came face to face with the dressed up panhandler and give his apology. From there, he would offer what he could.

He was two blocks from Elm Street and entering forbidden territory for the second time that night. Sam quickly spotted what he came to see –but something was peculiar. The weary figure had left its corner and was straggling across the street. This gave him the impression that the homeless man actually had a place to go to.

How right he was.

Sam walked down Main Street as Elmo disappeared going down Elm. The teenager walked fast to the corner of Elm Street just in time to watch something that added to the confusion. The midnight hobo entered The Men of Miner Fellowship Hall, closing the door behind him. This was another place expressively forbidden by his father. Sam was well behind enemy lines and went for broke. It was as if he was answering a calling.

He walked to the edge of the illuminated plate glass that exposed the entire hall and peered inside. What he saw was a cluster of his dad's friends surrounding the man in the outfit. He held his breath as the black gloves came off and set on the empty table next to him. Strong hands that seemed familiar were exposed. The suspense mounted as the hat came off next and placed with the gloves. Now came the grand finale; it was time to see who Elmo was.

The mighty hands reached up and grabbed the black ski mask. In one motion it was pulled off exposing an unmistakable bushy beard with graying hair. Sam was in shock and his whole world changed forever.

He found out who Santa Clause was.

Chapter VIII

SAM LAY AWAKE ALL night with his stomach in knots. He kept
looking around his bedroom realizing how fortunate he was. He
glanced out his window and viewed the icicles. Further away he
saw the rolling hills covered with snow and wondered how
anyone could survive out there. Guilt was taking its toll.

He played back in his mind over and over again how the
unknown panhandler tried to protect himself from the snowballs.
Sam wondered if it was his own father trying to defend himself
while he and his friends pelted Elmo.

He thought of the many nights when his dad would leave home
and not be seen until the following day. Again and again his mind
played back watching his father take off the black ski mask. The
look of shame his father's face held while trying to preserve his
dignity would forever be engrained in his mind.

He glanced around his room again taking a closer look at his
possessions. This time it was through the eyes of an adult. There
were posters and toys that nurtured dreams with expensive
clothing to compete with peers. All had nothing to do with the
bond of family love and the reality of surviving. They were still,

however, provided by his father because of the juvenile importance Sam held for them.

The son was opening his eyes. He decided to become allies with the breadwinner of the house and would take the fight to his dad.

It was Sunday morning with the ritual of attending church services mandatory. Sam liked going to church. It bridged gaps in only a way God could, further extending the path his father was trying to teach. He was always proud when his family entered the sanctuary. Later, they would discuss what they learned over lunch. He would utilize this special morning as a trump card to launch his campaign.

Sam noticed the time and realized that soon his mother would be in the kitchen.

The teen's thought process was now redirected with the boy getting out of bed and dressing in a hurry. *He* would make oatmeal for the household including a pot of coffee and even set the table. His goal was to give his parents a running start and pleasantly greet his father when he came downstairs.

Sam was busy working in the kitchen when his father awoke. Ben didn't sleep much and quietly got out of bed as to not disturb his wife. In moments, he was walking down the stairwell in his bathrobe and detected the aroma of fresh coffee. Ben was fully aware of what he was walking into.

The dad walked into the dining room and saw his son sitting at the table facing him. Sam was staring up at him like *Eddie Haskell.* The table was noticeably dusted with Ben's favorite mug placed on a coaster with steam rolling out of it. "Hey," greeted Sam in a joyous tone. "You're up early today."

Ben pulled out the chair assigned to him and sat down to watch his son's performance. He picked up the mug with both hands and took a drink of coffee. Next, he rested his elbows on the table holding the mug in front of his chin. Ben's eyes peered through the steam giving undivided attention. Sam was nervous. He avoided the possibility of a silent treatment and initiated a topic. "You know dad," he said with an intellectual expression, "I was just thinking..."

Ben was starting to become amused and continued to watch.

"That glove of mine doesn't need replacing after all," said Sam. "In fact, most of my favorite players kept the same glove for most of their careers," he added. The boy was fast on his feet and shifted gears. "Mom sure makes great lunches for Susan and me for school."

Ben could see the correlation he was trying to convey and mercifully put an end to it. The rugged dad spoke. "So you found out about me."

Sam started to fidget.

The big man placed his mug on the coaster and stood up extending his arms on the table. Leaning towards the boy he said with his baritone voice, "And I found out about you."

Sam knew what his dad was referring to. In a surrendering voice he said, "Sorry dad."

"Do you know why we're doing this charade?" asked the father.

With an innocent look Sam nodded his head slowly several times.

Ben was a very wise man and sat back down to address his son. "I've given this a lot of thought," he said with gentleness. "I felt that in time you would come to your senses and go back there to make amends. I also didn't think that your friends would join you." Looking at his son with the warmth of a father he asked, "Is that how it played out last night?"

Sam was sniffling like a child and nodded up and down several times.

"Do any of your friends know about our secret?" asked Ben. Sam shook his head as he fought back the tears.

"Well that's good," said Ben. The man of the house leaned back in his chair and continued to address his son. "You see, son," he continued with a passive tone. "Yesterday I sat in the bleachers watching you be a man in front of other men." He paused and took a sip of coffee. "That's how I know you. Last night you were suckered into peer pressure and made a mistake," he said pointing a finger at his son. "That's not who Sam Skates is."

Ben crossed his arms and continued. "I knew you'd be back eventually to do the right thing; I just didn't realize that it would be so soon that you would discover what my fellowship hall has been doing at night."

Sam stared at his father with respect.

Ben continued the one-sided conversation. "There is a part of me that's ashamed of you, but most of me respects you now more than ever." The righteous father got out of his seat and walked over to his son. With his strong arms he leaned over and hugged the boy saying, "Maybe involving you is just what the hall needed."

Ben walked back to his chair and sat down. "Dad," asked Sam in a somber tone. "Did it hurt?"

Ben looked at Sam and said, "You'll have to ask Pete; he was the guy that was out there." The father looked up in thought and placed his index finger on his chin. "He did say one thing, though."

Sam focused on his father as he prepared to hear the report.

"Pete commented that one particular snowball came at him with the velocity fit for the majors," said the father in a philosophical tone, "and that impressed him very much."

Sam appreciated his father's humor realizing that it was laced with an understanding. Teary-eyed, Sam broke into a chuckle. "Thanks dad," he reciprocated. "I'll make it up to him, too" he vowed. "I'll make it up to all of you."

"I know you will," said the father.

Sounds were coming from upstairs. Soon, the women of the house would be downstairs for breakfast. Ben looked at his son and said, "We have to keep this a secret from them."

"Don't worry, dad," assured Sam. "I won't tell anyone."

Gloria and Susan walked into the dining room wearing matching pink bathrobes. The mother said, "Is that coffee I smell?"

Ben responded, "More than that, there's oatmeal too." The father looked at Sam and said, "Someone around here is taking extra care for others." Sam got the double meaning and blushed at his father.

Gloria only understood that her son took the liberty to make breakfast. "Thank you," she said as she hurried towards the boy. The mother hugged Sam with both arms and kissed him on the head. "You are such a good son."

"I'll serve the oatmeal and get you some coffee mom," said Susan.

"Thank you, darling," replied Gloria. The woman of the house sat up and made a perplexed facial expression that got everyone's attention. "Is this Mother's Day?" she asked.

The family laughed at the comment and Ben said, "If it isn't, it is now."

Sam realized the happiness he created. He looked over at his dad and received a wink that verified he was on the right track.

"We need to make sure that we get to church on time," reminded Gloria. The family united with Ben leading the table in grace. The nutritious meal with milk, raisins, and brown sugar was enjoyed with Sunday morning off to a good start.

Church was just one block down and one over from their home; this justified walking which included escorting Sharon Wilson. Sam maintained his good form and personally went to her front door to assist her. "Bless you, Sam," said the neighbor on social security. Ben liked what he saw.

Cautiously, the quintet strolled on the polished ice like carolers during the holidays. The Puritan-white cathedral with stained glass came into view as they rounded the corner. A tall wrought iron steeple towered over the neighborhood, telegraphing its heavenly refuge. Two wooden doors divided down the middle resembled a castle from the sixteen hundreds. They were propped wide opened with glorious organ music carrying through the aisles and filling the street. Faithful parishioners entered the safe haven with Pastor Everett and Troy Meeker standing just inside. The clergymen who wore matching black suits with white shirts and pink ties greeted all who entered.

Sam knew that Troy was his dad's best friend. He watched his dad approach Pastor Everett first with his hand extended. The 61-year-old spiritual leader with thin gray hair parted to one side peered through his glasses in delight. Using both hands he clasped Ben's and said, "It's so good to see you here, brother Ben."

Ben used his free hand to pat the pastor on the back. "It always makes my day to see you, Pastor," he said with sincerity.

Sharon followed next with the rest of the Skates family behind. Ben stepped towards Troy and leaned towards his ear whispering, "Sam knows about everything." Troy nodded with the understanding. Sam noticed the brief interaction and knew what was shared. Troy looked at Sam's inquisitional face and gave a bright-eyed smirk that telegraphed, "So, you found out about us."

Sam volleyed back with a slight-head motion that resembled him on the mound. The five entered the lobby with Troy inconspicuously giving Sam a nudge on the shoulder.

After service, the family walked back through the lobby and greeted the many friends that attended. Sam watched his dad approach Troy from behind and rest his right arm over Troy's shoulder. The buddy elbowed back as laughter exchanged. Then he saw something that left an impression. Troy was holding two folded bills and placed them in his father's pen pocket. His dad's face showed a look of surprise with Troy giving him an okay sign with his right hand. Ben dropped his arms and then hugged his friend for the gift. That exchange showed Sam how bad things actually were for his dad.

Walking home, the family took turns visiting with Sharon Wilson. The short walk soon left off in front of the old lady's home. Susan followed her brother's lead by offering to walk Mrs. Wilson up her walkway to her front door. "Do you mind if your father helps me this time?" asked the feeble woman in a worried voice.

Sam was now more observant and knew what that meant.

"That sounds good," said Ben in a warm tone. "Susan," called out the dad, "you'll get to do it next time."

"Okay, dad," said Susan as she wrapped both arms around the senior. "Bye Mrs. Wilson."

The old woman of the neighborhood was touched and relieved. Patting both hands on Susan's back she said, "Bye-bye Susan. You and your family are so nice to me."

Next came Gloria's hug. "We love you so much," she said as they embraced.

"I love you too," said Sharon.

Sam was last. He hugged his neighbor and said, "It was great going to church with you today."

Embracing the teenager she tearfully said, "I love going to church with you too."

It was almost time for the private moment between the caring dad and the timid old lady. Gloria, Susan, and Sam continued walking home as they waved saying, "Bye!"

Mrs. Wilson waved back, "Bye!"

Ben walked Sharon to her front door as Sam watched from afar. He saw the old lady look down to get courage, then look up staring directly at his dad as she spoke. His dad's friendly gestures brought an immediate smile on the widow's face as he reached into his pen pocket. Sam could see clearly from where he was standing. True to form, his dad handed Sharon a bill. Gratitude was exchanged with a hug that utilized all of the senior's strength. She put the money in her purse and fondled for her keys. In moments, she was waving from her view window as a smiling Ben Skates waved back and returned home.

Sam was becoming more and more aware of how hard others were struggling to survive in that town. He was also overwhelmed on the strength his father possessed.

Sam was in his bedroom when a light tapping on his door got his attention. He opened it to see the ambassador of the house staring at him. "Can I come in and talk to you for a minute?" asked his father.

"Sure dad," answered Sam. "Come on in."

"Thank you," said his dad as he entered the bedroom closing the door behind him. He walked to the corner of the room and sat in a chair. With his hands on his lap he initiated a conversation. "Son," he spoke with directness. "The members of the hall made an agreement long ago to mention if any of our family members ever found out." With intensity, he asked a question that he asked earlier that morning.

"Now, Sam," repeated the dad. "Are you sure none of your friends know about what we're doing at nights by the freeway ramp?"

"Dad," said Sam. "Last night was the only time we ever went down there. My friends stayed behind when I went back and I haven't seen any of them since."

"Okay, Sam," said the father. "Troy did his duty by calling some of the guys and letting them know that you found out. He was supposed to tell the others, that's why I told him in church." Looking at Sam he continued. "I just talked to him on the phone and we feel that it's important that you come down to the hall and get a complete understanding on what's actually going on around here."

Sam perked up feeling accepted as an adult. "I'll be there dad."

"Good," said the father. "We will not go together in case your friends see us and decide to follow. Just be down there at seven tonight and make sure they don't know that you went there."

Sam loved being a part of the grownup side of the community and sharing secrets. "Don't worry, dad," he said. "I'll be there at seven and none of my friends will know a thing."

"Good," said the dad. He stood up and shook hands with his son. "See you at seven." The big man left the room and went downstairs.

Chapter IX

SAM DECIDED TO SPEND the rest of the day alone. He walked around town and soul searched by taking a good look at himself. The teen would also go a step further and evaluate the crowd he hung out with.

He changed out of his church clothes and dressed into the jeans and baseball jersey he normally wore. Wool socks accompanied tennis shoes that matched his school colors. He opened the top drawer of his dresser and grabbed a few dollar bills he always kept hidden in the far corner. Finally he dawned his letterman's jacket, combed his hair, and left the household undetected. Once outside, the fresh winter air engulfed the young man, promising the solitude he desired. He would spend the next few hours milling throughout the community with his innermost thoughts surfacing.

There was always something about his friends that made him feel a little out of place, a little *different*. He realized that what he did on Saturday night wasn't *him*. A valuable lesson would spawn from this however. One he would carry with him for life. Sam would never again compromise values based on peer pressure. He thought about the fellowship hall and was grateful that they were aware of his true character. It was the same character Ella pointed out earlier that evening. Once Ella came to mind, Sam directed his thoughts towards her.

He viewed her as not just a friend of the family, but *his* friend as well. Sam remembered that Ella always had time for him and gave sound advice when needed. The sun was setting and Sam felt a little weary. *A cup of hot cider sounds good right about now*, he thought to himself. Sam directed his travels towards the popular coffee shop and was soon entering through its front door. The young man always felt at home when he went to Ella's. This visit however, would be tainted.

"Well look who's here," came a distinct voice from across the room. Looking over, Sam could see the crowd he usually hung out with. At that moment he remembered the wisdom Ella shared with him the night before. She pointed out how they acted different when he was not with them and explained that his image helped theirs.

Familiar jacket and jersey combinations were staring at him along with friends that wore plain clothing. With the exception of numbers that gave personal identification, Sam felt mirrored by Ryan and Tim. Paul Muller was *just there.* Jeff Turner seemed to be the only true friend in the group. He seemed comfortable being himself. The others looked at Sam with concern. Jeff simply gave an open hand wave with his customary lean and smile.

"I called your old man today and he said you weren't around," said Ryan. "What's the matter?" he asked. "Are you too good for us?"

Sam looked away feeling attacked. His eyes met with Ella who was watching the one-sided exchange take place. She quietly answered Ryan's question by nodding her head up and down. That moment gave Sam a surge of energy.

The baseball star got in gear and approached the table. "We did something bad last night and it's been bothering me," he said.

"You are right," agreed Jeff. "I thought about it all night and feel disgusted with myself."

"That's how I feel," said Sam. "I couldn't sleep last night thinking about it."

Ryan challenged Sam's popularity. "Well I slept just fine," he said talking like a baby.

Tim stayed neutral. He looked up to Sam Skates and wanted to be just like him. He was also on the team and didn't want to be caught in the crossfire.

Paul remained quiet knowing that Sam was the man of the group.

Ryan stood up with authority. "Look, that was just a bum who uses people."

"That was a person that we didn't know and attacked," countered Sam.

"I agree with Sam," said Jeff. "Whoever that person was didn't deserve what we did."

"Are you blaming me for this?" asked Ryan in defense.

"No," said Sam as he lowered his head. "I am blaming myself. I knew better and could have stopped it." Looking up he saw a clock on the wall realizing that his meeting would start in twenty minutes. Nothing more needed to be said with Sam feeling more like a man. For the second time in twenty-four hours, he walked away from his peers.

Ella loved what she saw. With perfect timing she approached the booth asking, "May I take your order?"

Sam went outside to walk the dark streets. He felt tension as he repeated his trek to the fellowship hall. This time he was to be expected. Looking towards the freeway ramp he saw Elmo shivering with sign in place. Sam was now entering the territory where the *real* men of Miner hung out.

The high school kid reached Elm Street and promptly took a left. He passed several boarded up doors and found himself in the shadows of The Men of Miner Fellowship Hall. Sam looked at the faded wood door with the dull brass knob. Looking down, he held his breath and entered.

He took one step in the old landmark and noticed its faded wooden floors. Faint odors from a century's worth of gala events engulfed his surroundings. Footprints updated the room from those that presently frequented the dusty hall. Sam felt vibes knowing that he wasn't alone. Cautiously he closed the door and looked up.

There before him sat over thirty men he recognized. They were all staring at him with blank expressions. Sam was overwhelmed and looked back in silence. Finally a cheerful voice spoke up. "That's quite an arm you have there." It was Pete Rainwater, a grownup who Sam considered a friend. The personable Native American stood up rubbing his left shoulder and motioning the arm at the same time. "I could hardly move it this morning when I got up!" he said in a complimentary tone.

"That's because he's a Skates!" cried out Red Pennington as all heads turned to him. The former World War II veteran leaned forward and continued, "I used to watch his grandfather pitch right here in town. He was a sensation!"

Sam didn't know how to take the comment. He looked back at Pete and Red with a Cheshire grin. Ben Skates took control and stood up. "Son," he said in a commanding voice. "It's important that you understand what's going on around here."

Sam's face cringed as he addressed his father. With a jittery voice he said, "I think I have an idea."

At that moment, the boy on trial got the scare of his life. A cold black glove came from behind and grabbed his shoulder. Instinctively, he flinched and turned around to see Elmo staring at him face-to-face. "Boo!" projected the disguised hobo in a loud, sharp tone. Sam's arms and legs involuntarily twisted as he shook with fright. He leaped back with bulging eyes looking at the monster.

The entire room doubled up with laughter for a marathon five minutes. Sam turned to the captive audience and saw the humor. It was clear that they watched their friend enter the room and quietly sneak up on him. He couldn't help but laugh himself. "Glad you could make it," said a muffled voice behind the mask.

Elmo patted him on the back and walked to the urn to deposit the donations he begged and scavenged for. Sam watched the procedure as a clanking sound echoed throughout the room. The baseball star nodded in approval. He understood the genius that came from teamwork and appreciated seeing it applied in real life. The man dressed in the costume made his way to the chair in front of the portable heater and sat down.

Suspense mounted with Sam wanting to know who was behind the mask. The leather gloves and hat came off and were placed on a nearby table. The exposure allowed for better dexterity as shaking hands reached out in front of the heater. Slowly, they opened and closed with the palms almost touching the red-hot coils. A tingling feeling started to awake the beggars hands as he rubbed them together. Medicating heat continued to revive the trembling fingers as circulation increased.

The red swollen hands could now function better and reached up, grabbing the black woolen mask from the neckline. It was pulled off swiftly and tossed next to the hat. An exhausted familiar face had been revealed, satisfying the pleasantly surprised teen. It was none other than Troy Meeker himself; another adult who was also *his* friend. The self-sacrificing man with red hair extended his arm. With open fingers he tapped on Sam's shoulder saying, "If I could pick anyone out there to help us it would be you."

The 17-year-old was flattered to hear that. He was fully aware that Troy would never have said that if he didn't mean it. Another voice came from behind. "Hey Sam."

The boy looked behind and matched a hospitable face with the voice. It was another friend: Gene Fletcher. He was holding up a multicolored basket filled with treats and offered, "Grab some candy, we've got plenty."

"Thanks," replied Sam as he reached over and grabbed a handful of jelly beans and nuts.

Sam was beginning to feel more accepted. He appreciated who was there. He was also blessed because of who wasn't. Jake West was out of town to address a family matter. His competitiveness through his son, Ryan, would have thrown a wrench into the evening. Another time would be more appropriate for the insecure man to accept Ben Skates' son into the fellowship.

More voices were directed at the Skates boy followed with random pats on his shoulders and back. Sam looked around the yellow walls with dusty beams and felt at home.

"Son," called out the father. "This is the right time to explain to you what this hall is actually doing."

"I have already figured out what's going on here," said the perceptive teen.

"Why don't you tell us?" asked Cecil Parks. Sam looked at the fellowship and saw that he had the floor. The high school standout started to get out of his chair when Cecil directed him. "You don't have to stand up and give a formal presentation," he said. "Nothing here is formal; you are fine right where you are." Sam sat back down and stared at his lap. He spent a few precious seconds searching for the words needed to convey his thoughts. He was ready and looked up at the fellowship members.

"I need to apologize first," he said as his eyes scanned the room. "I knew better than to do what my friends and I did last night." Pausing, he maintained his composure while looking at every man in the room.

Pete Rainwater's hand rose. Sam was impressed with the respect that was shown throughout the room. Like his favorite teachers in school, Sam gave a nod handing the floor to Pete.

The Navaho eyes with high cheekbones spoke. "Sam," he said, "everyone in the hall was amazed that we lasted so long out there without being victimized by a high school prank. We credited you for that." The father of three continued. "You were just being a teen, but you are also Sam Skates. We expected you to return, but alone." Pete raised his right arm and pointed at him. "We have been steadily going downhill and having an additional Skates around here could only help."

Sam looked at his dad and received his patented inconspicuous wink. The young man was on fire and continued. "All of my friends are aware that times are hard around here; we just thought that this was higher ground than the rest of the state."

Looking eye to eye at each person individually, Sam elaborated further. "I guess deep inside I wondered how we could afford the things we still had. We never went hungry and on occasion, even got to go out for a treat. I now know why the poverty spreading throughout this valley didn't appear obvious to my friends." He saw the fathers of that small town waiting to hear his answer. He gave it. "It's because this hall was secretively getting handouts at night and helping the needy families that live here." The strong youth turned towards his father and finalized by saying, "And that included our family."

Ben had a tear run down the side of his face. He nodded admitting that they too were struggling. Sam looked back with a reassuring look of support.

Glenn Holmes raised his hand with Sam motioning him to speak. "Sam," he began to ask. "How did you feel last night when you found out about us?" The man of the hour had plenty to say and wasted no time.

"Do you really want to know?" he volleyed back with a touch of humor. "It was the worst feeling I have ever felt in my whole life!" It was clear that all could identify with the boy's feelings. Facial expressions encouraged Sam to open up more.

Sam got in gear and began to explain in greater detail. "When I realized that dad and his friends were that panhandler we called *Elmo,* I cried like a baby."

Red Pennington raised his hand. Sam looked at the old-timer and gave him a gesture to speak. All eyes were on Red as his face tensed up with a confused look. *"Elmo?"* he asked. "Who's Elmo?"

Troy Meeker raised his hand to give the teacher the answer. "Go ahead, Troy," said Sam.

"I think that name comes from the street corner we stand at," said the intellectual deacon. "We occupy a corner off of Elm Street," he pointed out. "So, wouldn't a group of teenagers play with the name and refer to the person standing there as *Elmo*?"

"Very good, Troy!" congratulated Sam. The room broke out with laughter with heads looking at one another. They *got it*.

Troy smirked like a child as he pivoted his head around the room like a proud student.

Sam became more animated as he accounted for his actions yesterday. "We misinterpreted why someone would be standing there for such a long time holding a sign," he said. "We naturally thought that an outsider was being lazy and trying to take advantage of this town." The fellowship with folded arms nodded in understanding.

His eyes cast throughout the hall as he spoke more. "I realized after a while that what I did was wrong and that's why I returned."

Looking down, he took a hard swallow. He stayed calm and looked up again. "That's how I found out about what was really going on. All I can say is that I'm sorry and I will do whatever I can do for this fellowship."

Wilson Thomas raised his hand. "How did you feel last night when you went to bed?" asked the senior.

The boy addressed the room saying, "I never felt so sick in my entire life. I spent all night looking at the ice and snow outside and wondered what we'd do if we ever became homeless." Sam saw faces that shared the same fear. "I thought about my dad and anyone else who could be out there at that time and realized that they could be dying." The room was quiet in agreement.

Gene Fletcher raised his hands with his innocent brown eyes looking at Sam. Sam pointed at the truck driver. "Sam," asked the gentle giant. "Would you ever want your mother and daughter to go through what you went through last night?"

"No!" exclaimed the adolescent. "I would never want them to go through that."

"We all feel the same way," explained Gene in a humble tone. "That's why we do every trick we can think of to keep this from our families."

Sam was horrified over the thought of his mother and sister ever finding out. His pasty white face showed he understood the importance of being tight-lipped. "Well good," said Gene. "I know that we can count on you."

"It must be my time to get out there," said Cecil Parks.

"No," said Sam with conviction. "It's my turn."

"Don't you have school tomorrow?" asked Cecil.

"The seniors have this week off," said Sam. "It's a parent-teacher conference week with the senior breakfast and hayride tomorrow."

The room looked at Ben. He pointed at the hobo outfit and said, "Go on and get in it, son. We hope you have good luck out there tonight."

Sam sat on the bench that held the outfit and took off his shoes. He pulled the baggy pants over his jeans and changed into *Elmo*. Once dressed, he picked up the sign and went outdoors to his station. All heads turned to Ben with respect. Suddenly, Ben Skates noticed something that jarred a recent memory.

By the door he saw a medium sized man in a jean outfit holding a matching western hat. The tanned face featured dark eyes behind heavy black glasses. A regimented black crew cut dictated authority. He knew who he was looking at. It was Stanley Horton, the man that needed his last dollar. It was obvious that he attended much of the meeting—if not all. The strange man from another part of the country placed his hat on his head. Using his index finger he touched the brim, quietly acknowledging Ben. He left without the others ever knowing he was there.

Chapter X

SAM FELT LIKE A soldier deployed on his first mission. He was now the *point man* for The Men of Miner Fellowship Hall. Protected by the ghostly shadows of the Samson building, he paralleled the frozen terrain. Precariously, he shuffled in the oversized circus shoes that slipped and slid every step of the way. In the darkness, he focused on the cause and got mentally prepared.

Then came reality.

He was now exposed at the intersection of Main and Elm. The reflective environment of ice, frost, and snow was glorified by the moon and stars. Mankind's artificial sources further intensified the ground where he would stand as a beggar.

Sam stood at the crosswalk that led to the unmanned post across the street. Looking to his right he saw the fields and playgrounds where childhood dreams spawned from. To his left was the ramp that led to those dreams.

The all-star picture no longer felt like a commando. The loud outfit that clashed with the styles of yesterday made him resemble a kid trick or treating alone for the first time. The popular teen felt like a clown wearing an outfit he wouldn't be caught dead in. He also knew that by crossing the street he would upgrade to grownup status.

Sam confirmed that there was no traffic from either direction. He wanted to be removed from center stage as quick as possible and began to cross the intersection.

At that moment nature introduced itself. A blind shot of Arctic wind raced down the barren street whistling through the loose clothing his dad wore at nights. Unmerciful degrees of frost penetrated every opening in his body and created new ones. The blast carried a hue of frostbite burn as his body tensed in defense. Like the lone hiker in Jack London's *To Build A Fire,* he was oblivious to the signs that forewarned of the unforgiving force approaching.

The boy who lived in a warm house didn't heed the warning of rattling bare branches. He didn't respond soon enough to the foliage racing towards him like rats abandoning a sinking ship.

The terrified boy bent over using the flimsy cardboard sign as a shield. The vicious blast seemed to only be an introduction and subsided immediately.

Sam was initiated. He recovered from the cold slap in the face and bravely marched to his post.

The teenager who usually wore designer jeans with brand name sports shoes had been stripped of his stripes. He was now the lowest member of society: a panhandler that drew attention by default. The bum nobody wanted.

Sam's feet rested on thin soles that lay with the contour of the frozen ground. His gym socks lost what little insulation they had and became one with the elements. A continuous rocking motion was needed to maintain circulation that generated heat. Heat that instantaneously evaporated from the shivering body.

Sam felt like the man on the moon. He looked up and down the ice arena known as Main Street and couldn't find a soul. The only activity was glistening lights and the automated traffic light that rotated signals. The boy started to become mesmerized by the wintertime nightlife. It was the second part of the day and a world in all its own; one that was exclusively restricted to few animals and an occasional traveler.

Sam momentarily chose to forget about his pain and marvel at the tranquil beauty under the milky sky. He now had time to fully appreciate nature's ice sculptures amidst the undisturbed snowfields. Silence further enriched the desolate paradise. Sam thought to himself as he slowly looked around. *How ironic it is to be surrounded by such beauty that challenges life.*

The serenity was disturbed by the movement of light. The teen fishing for handouts looked at the ramp entering Miner. Lights from a vehicle grew in size and came to rest at the stop sign.

To his delight it was kind of car he was hoping for: a dented gold station wagon which appeared to be carrying an entire family. What was more important was that the local boy did not recognize the vehicle or its occupants. It all seemed too good to be true. These variables practically guaranteed one thing: that they arrived in town with money to get gas. That would also mean that they would have to leave the same way they came in. Sam was getting a more in-depth understanding of how well thought out his vantage point was.

Who else could better relate to his plight than a family in a run-down car? he thought.

The gold relic slowly moved forward and turned into town as Sam frantically held up the sign. He started to display his youth by jumping up and down; a tactic that would prove to work against him. His heart was pounding with adrenalin as he boldly got the attention of the passing travelers. He watched the smoky exhaust dissipate in the cold air as the car drove down the street.

The station wagon went through the green light and drove a few blocks, turning into the unmanned gas station. The anxious boy got his hopes up and placed the sign on the ground. He rubbed his hands in anticipation waiting for their return.

Sam watched the entryway to the gas station like a hawk. Soon, bouncing faded lights appeared and grew brighter as the vintage Ford came into view. The student was ready. He grabbed the sign and started to gyrate every way possible at the approaching vehicle. The traffic light aided him by turning red, prolonging his show.

Then came the moment of truth. The light changed with the car beginning to accelerate towards the freeway ramp. Sam exerted everything he could muster up to be rewarded an offering of *any* size. The unknown occupants increased their speed and continued their journey. It was as if they never saw him. A dejected Sam dropped his arms and slumped forward. He felt like a candidate that answered every question right and still didn't get the job.

His isolation was interrupted by the revving sound of a an engine that echoed music as it traveled. He knew who it would be and why they were coming. Sam was on the verge of being attacked by the group he defected from. He didn't register any fear though; it brought out his anger instead. He stood proud and refused to hide.

The dilapidated brown pickup slid on the ice stopping in front of Sam. This time they had fewer members. Not only was Sam standing in disguise outside the truck, but Jeff Turner was a no-show. This made Sam stand even taller like an amused superman facing machine guns.

Ryan West had a different view. The clique might have lost its two most respected members but in turn, Ryan was advanced to top dog. The outfielder stood alone in the truck's bed and called out his battle cry. "Hey Elllmmooooo, get a job!"

Ryan unknowingly threw a snowball that ricocheted off of Sam Skates' left shoulder. The high school boys did a doughnut in the intersection and raced back to town honking the horn in victory.

Sam looked across the street and saw the men from the hall race towards him. Immediately he yelled out, "Don't worry; I'm okay."

That announcement stopped the men in their tracks. "Why don't you come in for a minute?" called out a voice.

The scout willfully walked across the street. Hands patted him on the shoulder as he walked to the hall. Once inside he placed the sign on a nearby table. Next, he removed the hat, mask, and gloves and set them next to the sign. Sam was faced by the masses as his dad spoke, "We saw everything," he said out of breath. "Are you alright?" he asked.

Sam started to laugh out loud. "Are you kidding?" he yelled. "Mom can throw a lot harder than that!"

"Did they find out who you were?" asked his dad.

"No dad," reported the son. "I'm not one of them anymore. I'm one of you."

Ben Skates hugged his son. "I know that you're upset with them and want to get even," said Ben. "But you can't let them know it was you out there tonight."

"Don't worry about it dad," said Sam using an intellectual tone. "This week we have an exhibition at the batting cage for more college scouts. I'll just tell the coach that the ball got away from me." Sam started to laugh at his own joke. "After all," he continued with a giggle, "Ryan needs to understand that baseball teaches life."

The room responded.

"Let him have it!" yelled out Red Pennington.

"I would hate to be him," said Cliff Hammond.

"Do it!" cried out Gene Fletcher. "That boy is overdue to be taught a lesson." More jeers and encouragement stirred up the room.

Ben extended his arms and placed his hands over Sam's shoulders. His piercing brown eyes looked directly at his boy with a slight grin giving approval.

"Let's get you out of that outfit," said Jon Schultize. "I think it's my turn now."

Sam refused. "Not yet," he said in a prideful tone. "I still have some time out there." The young man put the mask, hat, and gloves back on and carried the sign back to his station.

Ben turned around and faced the room. His face was red as he laughed to himself in astonishment.

Sam Skates was back on his watch. Quickly the intense chill of late night February encompassed him. Repetitive motion fought the frost in a losing battle. Seldom, a vehicle would pass through town to fuel up. Sam would do his part to make his presence known, but to no avail. He realized that out there, you're either lucky or you're not.

He was beginning to get tired and found himself almost falling asleep while standing up. Listing from side to side to stay warm and praying for a handout of any size, the warrior began to question if it was worth it. Sam wanted to return to the hall a victor but he was failing that night. Tears started to flow inside the mask from the athlete who never lost.

Unexpectedly, the weight of a large hand pressed down on Sam's shoulder, startling him. He turned around and was relieved to see his friend Pete looking at him. "You've got to try some of my stew," he said. "I saved some just for you." Sam's knight in shining armor arrived just in time. Sam was cold and hungry but at that moment he needed a friend. The man who always knew 'when to be where' put his arm around the boy and walked him to the hall.

Eleven o'clock found 43-year-old Bill Freeman playing *Elmo* with Sam stretched out in front of the portable heater. His hands were being warmed by a porcelain mug that held Pete's renowned stew. Next to him was a small dinner tray with two buttered rolls on a paper plate and a cup of cider. He savored the nutritious meal as he got better acquainted with common faces he saw around town.

Eventually he was sitting next to his father. "Well, what do you think son?" asked his dad. Sam looked around the room and studied the few members that were still present. The boy perked up and said, "This place is great, dad."

Ben patted his son on his lap and said, "I'm glad you like it."

"Hey dad," he asked in a lower voice. Ben leaned over to listen better. "These guys must love it here. It's almost midnight and there are still a few guys visiting."

Ben cleared his throat to give his son vital information. "They are not visiting," he quietly said. "They have been forced to stay here because their homes got foreclosed on." Sam looked at his dad in shock.

"This hall houses those who need a place to live," said his dad. "Every week we seem to get one of two more residences here. This town is slowly folding up and they don't have anywhere else to go." Ben gently slapped his son on his lap and walked away. He wanted the message to sink in.

It registered with Sam as he leaned back in his chair in disbelief.

Chapter XI

SAM WOKE UP AT eight thirty Monday morning. He was allowed the luxury of sleeping in being a senior that year. The student was facing the last stretch of high school with the traditional senior breakfast to start in a half hour. Later in the day would be the senior hay ride followed by a dance that evening.

The four year letterman briefly laid in bed reflecting on the night before. Many events took place that evening, but one stood out above the rest. It was the man-to-man talk he had with his father while walking home. It was expressed to him explicitly over and over again to keep the fellowship hall secret from the family and especially his friends. Sam was constantly reminded of the stress and anxiety *he* went through once he found out. A pain he wouldn't want to share with his mother, sister, or even his worst enemy. His dad was lowering his guard as a father and beginning to address his son as a friend. He mentioned how he looked forward to Mondays. He shared how blessed he felt having at least three days of work and confessed that those first three days of the week were when he felt like a man. Sam was happy for his dad that it was Monday morning.

The student hopped out of bed and showered. He changed into his after school clothes and combed his hair in front of the mirror.

Looking out his upstairs window he got distracted. Sam saw his dad outside talking to his best friend, Troy Meeker.

Something was wrong. His father was animated like an Italian opera star performing on stage. He pranced around with non-verbal language illustrating that an injustice had just taken place. Troy placed his hand on his dad's shoulder to calm him down. The deacon then opened his hand and placed two folded bills in his father's shirt pocket. His dad was obviously stymied over the news he just received and having to accept another handout. Sam saw his dad come to his senses and stand up straight like a soldier. Facing his friend he relaxed, accepting the situation.

Sam didn't have to be told what happened. He knew that his dad became a statistic and lost his job.

There was more to the picture.

The bed of the truck was heavily loaded with firewood. A closer look showed the crew cab filled with sacks of food he noticed in the fellowship hall the night before. Troy said something to his father with his dad nodding his head repetitively. Sam watched his dad become energized. He raced around the vehicle and climbed inside.

Sam knew how they thought. It would be a day where Troy and Sam's dad would play 'Santa Clause' for the less fortunate in the community. This was the only way Sam knew his dad. When he wasn't working, he was serving.

The only son was hit hard from what he just saw. He noticed the time and left for the celebrated breakfast.

Ben and Troy were on the same page as they traveled down the road. "How about dropping by Chester and Marian's place first?" suggested Ben.

"That's a good place to start," agreed Troy. The two-man work force went down Main Street and turned into the block where the Carltons lived. The truck familiar to the entire community parked in front of the elder couple's house. "Does the church have any extra paint?" asked Ben as he looked at the faded green house that was peeling.

"We certainly do," replied Troy.

"I bet we can cover that house in two days when it gets warmer," said Ben.

"I challenge you to that bet," said Troy as he extended hands, shaking Ben's to confirm a non-profit contract.

Looking at the house, they saw the surprised elder couple in front of their view window. They waved while being supported by their walkers.

Ben and Troy got out of the truck with Troy grabbing two bags of food. Ben added to the generosity by taking a small bundle of dried wood as a sample. Together they walked to the front door bearing the gifts.

It took time, but Chester eventually opened the door. The proud man peered through his glasses, protecting his wife behind him.

Ben spoke first. "How much do you want?" he asked as he displayed the firewood with both arms.

Marian rolled alongside her husband as they looked at Ben's loaded arms. Gazing at one another, the man and wife relished the idea of having a cozy fire at night. Chester looked at Ben and took command. "As much as you're willing to give us."

Ben's polished teeth gritted through his rugged beard. *This* was what made him happy.

Troy chimed in with his compassionate voice. "Don't forget these," he said as he held up the grocery bags. Chester and Marian were elated and invited them in.

"I'll make some tea," said the 88-year-old woman.

"Let me help you," offered Troy. The woman pivoted in increments and cautiously rolled towards the kitchen. The former Eagle Scout followed her with bags in hand.

Ben addressed Chester. "Where would like your wood?" he asked.

"Follow me," said the elder. Gracefully, he slowly backed up, turned around, and maneuvered towards the fireplace. Ben was led fifteen feet to the brick enclosure with leaded glass shutters. Brass handles matched the empty frame next to the fireplace that once held wood. Ben inspected the situation and said, "Let me take care of this while your wife is making tea."

Chester might have been old but still had some vigor. He raised his right hand and gave a spirited thumbs up. Ben could only smile back with respect. He went outside realizing that it would require several trips to fully supply the household. As he started to reach towards a piece of wood, a hand came from nowhere and grabbed it. He was caught off guard and looked over to see who it was.

To his surprise he was staring at a reflection of himself many years ago. Looking back was the fresh look of his own son.

"Son," he said with a puzzled expression. "This is your day; you're supposed to be out with your friends."

Sam had an immediate response. "This *is* my day and I am going to spent it with a friend."

Ben received the best compliment a father could ever hear. His son had the option to hang out with any friend at any place and still chose to be with him. Ben clenched his mighty fist and gently pressed it against the boy's head. Blushing from flattery he said, "Well let's get some wood in there."

"Okay dad," answered the enthused teen.

The addition of Sam constituted a party by golden year's standards. The local celebrity who was written up in the newspapers had fanfare in that household. He was briefly introduced to the couple and then assisted his dad until the rack was fully loaded. Next the fireplace was cleaned out with a boy scout campfire ready to go.

The necessity of food and heat to survive the winter had been provided with another important issue being addressed. The crime of not spending quality time with seniors would never be allowed here.

Tea time arrived with Sam receiving Chester's attention. "I remember watching your grandfather play," he said. "He was the greatest pitcher I have *ever* seen." Sam was proud of his heritage and beamed at his father. Ben relished what he heard and winked back.

Troy elected not to contribute to the conversation. He was enjoying too much of what he was watching. On occasion his eyes would meet with Ben's. The visit lasted close to an hour with the trio explaining that they had to leave to assist other families. Gratitude was expressed many times over with promises being made for future visits; promises that would be kept.

The Three Musketeers valiantly combed the small town delivering to every struggling household they knew of. They worked diligently until such families were visited and all supplies were gone. It was close to dinner time as Troy dropped Ben and Sam off in front of their house.

Before leaving the vehicle, Ben invited Troy to have dinner with them. "I'd love to," he said. "But as you know my mother needs me now."

"Then we'll just have to have both of you over," said Ben.

"We'd love that," said Troy. "Thanks for the help, Ben," he added. "And that goes for you too, Sam."

"I loved it!" said Sam. "I hope to see you later tonight, bye." The young man left the truck and ran to his house.

Ben was alone with Troy. He patted his pen pocket and humbly said. "I appreciate what you gave me today."

Troy looked at Ben with admiration. Then he livened up the moment by grabbing his friend's shoulder and shaking it. In a rambunctious tone he said, "You are worth it and a lot more, Mr.!" That action loosened Ben up a bit as he smiled back in appreciation.

"See you at the hall tonight," said Ben.

"I'll be there," assured Troy.

Ben Skates got out of the truck and walked to the dinner that awaited him. Throughout the meal, he and his son enjoyed the gathering without mentioning anything that could incriminate them. After the meal Sam and his sister did their chores while Gloria called a friend. Like clockwork, a light tapping on the front door could be heard.

Sam watched from the dining room as his father opened the door to greet Sharon Wilson. He noticed that she did not want to enter the home right away to keep their conversation private. He knew what would be next and he was right. His dad reached into his pen pocket and gifted a bill to their neighbor. She accepted it and placed it in her purse in one motion. Next, she accepted the invitation and entered the home.

Sam entered the room and hugged the senior. "It's great to see you, Mrs. Wilson," said Sam in an accommodating voice. Ben stood behind Sharon and watched his boy. The proud dad was pleased with the reception his son gave her and gave an okay sign with his fingers. The old lady loved being hugged by Sam and embraced.

"Oh, you're so sweet." she said patting him on the back. Within minutes, she sat comfortably in front of a fire sharing tea with the family she adopted.

After a short visit, Sam excused himself and went to his room. He changed into sweat pants with wool socks to prepare for the cold night. Before leaving his room, he opened the top drawer of his dresser and reached to the far corner. What little money he had hidden went into his pocket. Once downstairs he said goodbye to everyone. Sam glanced at his father before exiting the front door with his dad acknowledging back in silence.

The high school senior embarked to the fellowship hall. He walked past his school and saw the gymnasium decorated for the dance. At this stage of his life it all meant nothing to him. In his mind, he was in the adult world with high school far behind.

He approached the intersection of Elm Street and nonchalantly made a jest at *Elmo*. The bundled up fellowship member recognized the Skates boy and gave a slight wave back. Sam turned on Elm Street and was now off of the main drag. He still had the hobo's attention and pointed at his wrist watch. Sam motioned to the figure to end his shift. Elmo gave a 'why not' shrug and returned to port.

Once inside the heated room, Sam turned to see who was he was replacing. Elmo entered just behind him and placed the sign on the table closest to the door. He walked to the urn and deposited a muffled clanking sound that indicated paper money laced with coins. Then he walked to the designated chair in front of the portable heater and sat down.

The thrift store hat was removed and placed on the table next to him. Black gloves slowly reached up to the mask and pulled it off with the snap of the finger. Exposed was the jolly face of Jesse Richards, the town's only barber. The late model citizen with wild blue eyes and thinning gray hair made a funny face with his tongue sticking out. He showed that he could still make the boy who once needed a board resting on the arm rests giggle. Sam giggled at the court jester that watched him grow up.

The boy was better dressed for the night and put on the costume as pieces became available. Once fully dressed, he grabbed the sign knowing that *there is gold in them there hills!* He ran out to try his luck once again. "Go get 'em!" cried out a voice as he left the hall. Sam was at his post in record time.

His luck would change with a twist added. The senior hayride was driving down Main Street. A John Deere tractor pulled the antique hay trailer that had a three foot retaining wall wrapped around it. It was lit up with white Christmas lights and played party music. Inside was the graduating class amongst the hay bales. Gloved hands were holding caramel apples and steaming cups of cider. It was driving all the way through town to climb the snowy fields one last time.

The float drove by Sam and then stopped. Coins were thrown his direction with paper bills floating in the mix. There were no jeers, just sympathy. Sam remained speechless as he scurried for the bills that were floating away like ashes. The party moved on with the baseball standout incognito. He *knew* that he was not identified.

Across the street were hall members that watched the event. They were impressed for the dignity shown to their man on the corner, except for Ben Skates who just arrived. He watched his son act like a reject from society in front of the very school he attended. The father was disgusted with himself. He realized that his son was the school's prized student and should have been on the hayride and not in the gutter.

Sam didn't care about the classmates throwing money at him. His concern was to join forces with the fellowship hall and do his part to help the community. Ben couldn't stand it anymore and ran up to his son saying, "You have done enough for us tonight. I want you to go to the dance and have a good time."

Sam stood up and looked at his dad through the mask. "Are you sure, dad?" he asked.

"Yes, son," he answered. "Trust me, this is the best haul we've ever had out here. Besides, there are others in the hall who also want to take shifts." Putting his hand on his son's shoulder, he spoke with his warm voice. "Go to the dance, son. We've got everything covered tonight."

Sam interpreted his dad's message as a reward. He thought about it and realized that he would have a good time at the dance. "Gee, thanks dad!" exclaimed the teen.

"You've definitely earned it, son," he said. "But remember about keeping our secret," he cautioned.

"Don't worry dad," said Sam. "Let me finish picking up the money then I'll come in."

"Okay," said the dad patting him on the back.

The men were in the hall playing cards when Sam came in. He put the sign on the nearest table and placed the hat, gloves and mask next to it. Then he walked to his dad and started to empty out all of his pockets. A mound of shiny coins grew in front of Ben as his son continued to dig deeper into the pockets. An occasional dollar appeared along with two fives. "We should count it to see how much I got," requested Sam. The boy sat in front of the heater and began to change. Once out of the outfit, Shawn Clayton changed into it. The unemployed truck driver walked to the sign, picked it up, and left for the corner.

Sam was back in his clothes and reached into his pocket. He removed the money he had hidden in his dresser and walked to the pile of change that was almost counted, placing it next to it. In a minute the grand total was announced. "Hey," said Cecil Parks. "You broke my record! We have here sixty-two dollars and ninety-seven cents."

Sam was once again in his record setting form and left the hall with his arms up in victory. "Have a good time, son," called out Ben.

"I will, dad," he replied as the door closed behind him.

Ben stared at the change and got depressed. He was out of a job with his savings account soon to be emptied that week. He would now have to lobby at the unemployment office for another extension. He would once again search for work near and far and contact any friend or acquaintance for any lead. He would accept any work, anywhere, at any price. Ben Skates was within striking distance of being on welfare with the ugly reality of being homeless a distinct possibility.

Ben looked around the fellowship hall with the full awareness that it was progressively becoming a homeless shelter. *Who knows,* he pondered, *my family might have to live here soon.* The loose change in front of him was virtually worthless at that point.

His mind played back the noble effort his son gave. Watching him dressed as a shamed beggar in front of his peers churned his stomach. He viewed him as a courageous patriotic soldier that was fighting a losing battle to the death; a battle that would have no effect on the outcome and soon be forgotten.

Ben would trudge forward that night and serve his time on the corner. He would get a few strikes and a couple of close calls. Once relieved of duty, he would put the four dollars and seventeen cents into the brass urn and return home.

The following morning Sam woke up on cloud nine. He was much welcomed at the dance having missed the hayride. "I had to help my dad with something," was his excuse. He had wind in his sails from the money he panhandled for the fellowship and would now address another important matter. That afternoon he would be at the batting cage to pitch in front of more baseball recruiters. Ryan would also be there to display his batting skills.

It was shortly after twelve noon with the exhibition underway.

The great Sam Skates took to the mound as Ryan West stood at bat. Sam had a presence and was in control. He looked at the batter and saw the determined, overconfident look that always plagued the outfielder. He focused on the catcher and accepted his signal. Sam gripped the hardball by the threads. He wound up raising his leg high into the air and fired a missile. The spinning projectile initially seemed to be on target. In a millisecond it was already traveling too high and unexpectedly curved towards the batter. Ryan instinctively began to close his eyes and turn away as the...

Chapter XII

IT WAS AFTER DINNER at the Skates' residence with the table cleared and dishes put away. Sam was upstairs in his bedroom and eager to return to the hall; he was now living for the cause he had come to know.

In the meantime, Ben was reevaluating the situation. In doing so, he confirmed a frightening conclusion. He watched the town of Miner slowly dwindle as more of his friends lost their jobs, including himself. He did the math and realized that the money collected at the corner could not keep up with the sky-rocketing demand. When first started, the scheme put a dent into supplementing needy families, with seniors getting the lion's share. It was a necessary kick needed to enhance the fundraisers and private donations that kept their doors open.

Times had gotten worse with the local economy in a tail spin. Realistically, at best, the free money would only slightly delay the inevitable. At this point, the pillar of the community did not know what to do.

Ben was emotionally exhausted and needed a friend to lean on. Wisely, he chose his son. The dad went to the kitchen and brewed some coffee. Once done, he poured the hot coffee into two mugs and placed them on a tray. He took a spoon with some cream and sugar, placing the condiments and utensils next to the coffee. Gingerly, he picked up the tray and walked upstairs to the boy's bedroom door. Balancing the tray with one hand, Ben knocked.

Sam opened the door. His face lit up seeing that it was his father setting the stage for a dad and son talk. The son who rarely drank coffee studied the tray and saw the condiments provided. This illustrated that he was taken into consideration, further emphasizing their developing friendship.

"Can I talk to you for a while?" asked the dad in a diplomatic tone. "I'm drowning in problems and need someone to listen to me."

Sam was honored. He opened the door further inviting him in. Once he was in, Sam closed the door behind him. Ben walked to the nightstand and set the tray on top. "Would you like some cream and sugar with your coffee?" asked the father.

"Sure dad," replied Sam.

Ben put a mild dose of cream in Sam's coffee followed by a teaspoon of sugar. He stirred it and handed to him. "Sit down, son," said the father.

Sam took the mug thanking his dad. The boy went to the lounge chair in the corner of his room and sat while Ben went to the adjacent chair facing Sam. They each took a sip of the rich coffee. "This is good, dad," said the son.

"Glad you like it," replied the father.

Another sip was shared as the father gathered his thoughts. He put the mug on the edge of the dresser next to him and looked down, twiddling his thumbs for two seconds. The grown man was ready and looked up to address his son.

"Do you know how hard I try?" he asked his son.

Sam immediately injected. He leaned forward with a sincere expression and said, "Dad, you do it all; you make everything happen."

The father held out his right hand like a police officer stopping traffic. He needed to vent without any interruptions. Sam obeyed the request and remained quiet. Standing up he walked to the window and methodically gazed off into the distance. "I have made every sacrifice I could think of," said the father in a soft tone. Turning around he looked at Sam and continued, "But they didn't penalize me in any way. I actually liked walking around town instead of driving. It's also rewarding helping your mother make lunches for you and your sister." Sam watched as his dad exposed more feelings.

"Now, son," he said. "You and your sister have been wonderful throughout all of this. The two of you have not been a financial burden to this household." Ben continued. "Both of you have done your part to help your mother and I throughout these times." Sam leaned back in relief.

"What gets me," said the dad pacing the floor as he looked down, "is at my job we were working extra hours for free and even allowed our company to negotiate our contract. We were bending and giving as much as we could to secure what work we did have." Ben put his hands behind his back and stopped in his tracks. Looking to the ceiling he said, "And despite all of that sacrifice, they still tell us that they were forced to close us down because of the bad economy." The dad shook his head back and forth over the irony.

He was now going to ask his son a question. He sat back down and took a drink of coffee. Holding the mug with both hands he leaned back in the chair and looked at his son. "What am I overlooking?" he asked.

Sam had a suggestion.

"Dad," he said, "there is something that this family always does that I don't see the hall doing."

Ben was intrigued and placed his mug on the dresser. He motioned his right arm towards Sam and gestured to hear more.

"It's something we always do whenever we go camping," he said dropping clues. Ben was puzzled. He raised his right hand and gently pinched his chin with a contorted look on his face. Ben looked at his son and gave a blank stare that conveyed he still didn't know what he was referring to.

The son continued. "It's something we do before we go on a vacation," he hinted. Then Sam made it painfully obvious. "We even do it at home before bed time and especially before every meal."

It dawned on Ben what his son was getting at. He opened his hands and raised them outwardly as he looked up. His expression was that of *'why didn't I think of that?'*

The dad was enlightened as he got up and walked towards his son. Slapping him on the lap he said, "I need to go downstairs and make a phone call." Ben was elated that he wasn't quite painted in a corner yet. He put the empty mugs on the tray that held the spoon, cream, and sugar. Picking up the tray he left the room to contact Troy Meeker.

Sam stayed in his room feeling more instrumental to the fellowship hall. He would wait to hear from his dad.

Forty minutes later the father tapped on Sam's bedroom door and entered. "We're having a prayer visual tonight at midnight," whispered the dad. "Every member will be there. Get some sleep and I'll get you when it's time to go," he instructed.

Sam loved seeing his father rejuvenated. He was partaking in yet another strategy to save the community; a venture that had the highest connections. "Okay dad," said the son.

It seemed that immediately after Sam got in bed his dad was waking him up. "We have to go now," he quietly said rocking his son's shoulder. The dad and son team left the house a half hour before the meeting was to start. During their walk to town, an occasional car going to the hall would tap its horn to acknowledge them. Soon they arrived to a packed house. Troy intentionally bumped into Sam and said, "I knew you'd come up with something good."

All eyes looked at Ben and then to his son. Sam addressed the congregation. "Let's make a circle with everyone holding hands." The room followed his instructions. Once the circle was formed, Sam wasted no time initiating prayer. All bowed their heads as he called out "Dear Lord, we are here to serve you and ask for your guidance." The young man went into detail thanking God for what was already provided and asked for his blessings to allow more prosperity.

He was brief and to the point. Once he completed his prayer he, shook his left hand to queue the man standing next to him. One by one, each member contributed their prayer in the pecking order they stood in. Finally, the momentum made its way all around the hand-held circle leading up to the last and most respected man the town knew: Ben Skates.

Ben was ready as the group tightened their hands for the grand finale. "Dear Lord," spoke the big man, "we are here to ask you for more guidance and mercy." Ben Skates elaborated on how the town of Miner was always a God-fearing community that took care of its own. He expressed on how the citizens always united to survive and welcome others in need. "Lord, here we are out in the middle of nowhere," he pleaded, "please send your grace to this town immediately." Ben was finished with a chorus of

"Amen" following. Hands relaxed, letting go of their neighbor, and before anyone could look up a distinct voice called out.

"Excuse me, but did I hear you correctly?" All eyes turned to a medium sized man in a jean outfit. He was the same man who came and left the other night that only Ben noticed—the man who sat next to him in the gym knowing that he was down to his last dollar, as if conducting a test. "Did you say that we are in the middle of nowhere?" he questioned.

Ben looked at the eyes behind the dark prescription glasses. The inconspicuous authority figure with the dark crew cut stared back. "I did say that," replied Ben. "That's because we are precisely in the middle of nowhere; a place far away from everything else." He didn't know what to think of his new acquaintance. With curiosity he cautiously asked, "Who are you anyway?"

"My name is Stanley Horton," he proclaimed. "I am the director for The Middle of the Road Oil Company." The room was silent giving him undivided attention. "I was put on assignment by my company to travel this country and find where the middle of nowhere is," he said. "We want to build a super truck stop there that not only cater to trucks, but to families as well."

The entire room felt a tingling sensation throughout their body as they listened to the strange man. Each knew that this was truly a Godsend.

Stanley began walking around the room as he described what the truck stop would consist of. "This truck stop will supply fuel for any type of vehicle as well as having a restaurant, motel, coffee shop, automotive store, grocery store, and garage to repair anything that travels on the road. It will be an oasis for all who are far away from everything else. We will even have showers with a laundry mat there," he added.

There was more. "We don't just set up shop *anywhere*," he pointed out. "It has to be an American town that shares our values." Walking up to Ben he mentioned some of the statutes. "It has to be a place where the township would never allow someone to be hungry or become homeless. A place where a stranger has a place to stay and is always guaranteed a warm meal." Stanley reached into his shirt pocket and pulled out a dollar bill. He raised it high in the air and said, "It has to be somewhere where a man raising a family would give his last dollar to that stranger and open his home to him." Stanley placed the dollar back into its original owner's pen pocket.

Ben looked at Stanley realizing that he was being evaluated since the very beginning. Stanley winked at him and walked in front of the fellowship. "I have accomplished my mission," he proclaimed. "The middle of nowhere is right here in Miner."

"Please bear with me while I make a phone call," he said. Stanley Horton pulled out his cell phone and walked to an isolated corner of the room. His body language exemplified that he was engaged in an important conversation. The nodding of his head showed that he was having no complications with the party on the other end. Soon came an obvious sign of success; he raised his arms over his head and started to flex them like superman. He folded the cell phone and put it in his front pocket. Stanley turned around and walked back to the men who waited in silence.

Standing in front of the entire fellowship he spoke. "The Middle of the Road Oil Company has recognized the town of Miner as being the middle of nowhere. We have just committed ourselves to build a super truck stop right here in this very town and will hire all available local citizens first."

Wild cheers echoed throughout the hall with arms waving in excitement. The determined faces of The Men of Miner Fellowship Hall realized that they had won their battle. The town of Miner was saved!

Stanley Horton had more to say. "It is our policy to have the new employees' help with the construction," he said. "During this time, each employee will be paid one hundred dollars a day including one meal until the project is done." Heads turned to one another and nodded with approval.

"There is something else," he said getting everyone's attention. "We are a goal-oriented company that has deadlines and bonuses for making those deadlines." All breaths were held as to not disturb what Stanley had to say. The director for the oil company built up suspense as he scanned the room, looking at everyone eye to eye.

"I have faith that from what I have seen in this fellowship, I am absolutely convinced that we will make our deadline which is three months from groundbreaking. In fact, I am so sure that we'll make it that I am willing to gamble and pay each of you your bonus of two thousand dollars up front at this very moment." Standing back with his hands raised in the air he yelled out. "Are you with me?"

A huge ovation thundered throughout the room. One that eclipsed any event ever held in the history of the brick structure.

Stanley had a black leather briefcase laying on a chair and picked it up. He walked to a table and opened it saying, "I have applications for anyone looking for a full time job. My signature is even written down as your personal reference," he informed. "All I need you to do is to fill out the front page and sign it."

The men needing work formed a line in front of the oil representative. Each took an application and shook hands introducing themselves. They were given company pens that were red, black, and gray with the company logo on it. Within moments, each returned their form to Stanley. One by one the oil director reviewed each document and then wrote out a check for two thousand dollars.

Business was running smoothly as Stanley took the floor once again. "Construction will start once we have secured the property we want to build on," said Stanley. "In the meantime, I will coordinate job training and use Ben Skates as my contact." With assurance he finished by saying, "Ben will keep everyone informed. Thank you for your time; it has been a pleasure meeting everyone. We should be underway sometime this week." Stanley Horton picked up his briefcase and walked to a chair where his denim hat rested. He put the hat on his head and quietly left the room.

The hall started to empty with everyone following Stanley Horton's order. They would wait for a phone call to get further instructions. Once outside, Ben was affectionately pushed by Troy Meeker, causing him to gently bump into his son. "Didn't I tell you that Sam would come up with something?" said the red haired deacon.

Ben glanced over to his son and said, "You certainly did..."

Chapter XIII

BEN AND HIS SON were exhausted when they got home and fell
fast asleep. Ben was awakened first by his wife. "A man by the
name of 'Stanley' wants you to call him back at this number,"
said Gloria. She held a piece of paper with a ten digit number
written on it and placed it on the night stand next to the bed.

That message made Ben wide awake as he hopped out of bed and
put on his bathrobe. Gloria watched her husband quickly return
the call wondering what the importance was. She exercised
politeness by leaving the room. "This is Stanley Horton," were
the opening words Ben heard through the receiver.

"Stanley, this is Ben Skates," responded Ben.

"Ben," exclaimed Stanley. "I knew I'd hear from you soon. How
are you this morning?"

"I am fine, Stanley, and you?" he asked.

"I'm doing well," replied Stanley. "Ben," he said in a changed
tone. "Can I ask you for a favor?"

"Anything, Stanley," he answered.

"Can my company, I mean *our* company, conduct meetings for the next couple of weeks at your fellowship hall?" asked Stanley Horton.

Ben was honored. "Why, yes," he explained. "That hall is always open and you can schedule as many meetings you want as many times as needed."

"If that's the case," remarked Stanley, "then we can start the ball rolling tomorrow."

The company director addressed the ground he covered since their last visit six hours ago. Stanley confided that he carefully reviewed the filled out applications he received at the hall. He would now assign applicants to attend specific seminars that would serve as training based on what jobs they selected on their application. That week a training staff would begin to conduct meetings at the hall along with a buffet to accommodate the new employees.

Ben was given three lists of names and the times they were to report to the hall. He was also informed that within a day or two, the site for the new truck stop would be revealed.

"Thanks Stanley," said Ben in a gracious tone.

"No," said Stanley, "thank you." The congenial business man finished by saying, "You and the town of Miner are what we have been looking for. It's my pleasure to know you, Ben. I have to go now; I'll be calling you back in a day or two. Goodbye, Ben."

"Goodbye, Stanley," said Ben as he hung up the phone. He walked into the living room with an elated expression and addressed his wife. "You wouldn't believe what happened last night," he said.

"I got to hear this," she replied. "I'll get us some coffee and you can tell me all about it in the dining room."

Once they both sat down Ben tactfully explained that he lost his job and didn't mention it in case he found work soon. Gloria respected her husband's decision. Next, he started to tell about what happened at the fellowship hall. From there he told her about the prayer session led by their son and the involvement of Stanley Horton immediately following. He finished by telling her about the new truck stop being built and then he showed her his advanced bonus check.

"I'm so proud of you, Ben," said the tearful wife as she got up and hugged her husband.

Sam loved having the week off from school and enjoyed the late nights with his father. He had just woken up and come downstairs in time to see his dad display the bonus check. He watched his mom break into tears and embrace the man she loved. He decided it was best if he left the emotional moment undetected.

"Honey," said the husband. "I have to call Troy right away. Stanley has arranged meetings that the entire hall needs to attend."

"You go right ahead, Ben," she said. With loving eyes she kissed her man one more time. Once finished, Ben patted Gloria on the back and left to address business.

He took the cell phone and made contact with Troy, sharing the news with him. Names and meeting times were relayed, with an agreement on who would call what members.

Ben spent the next hour sitting in the living room calling the men assigned to him. He informed them about the meetings being conducted at the fellowship hall and what time they were to attend. They were also told of the buffet that would be catered. Once his calls were completed, he looked up to see his wife staring at him with pride. "I am going to cook a late breakfast for two hard working men I know of," she said. The thoughtful wife turned and walked to the kitchen.

Ben and Sam enjoyed the smoked ham and cheese omelets with rye toast covered in homemade raspberry jam. At that moment *they* felt like kings. "What are your plans today, son?" asked the dad.

"I'm not sure," he said. "I have a lot of friends out of school this week that I can call to do things with," he said. "How about you?" he asked.

"I was going to deposit my bonus check in the bank today and then go to the hall and tidy it up for the meetings tomorrow," said the father.

"I'll help you, dad," said Sam.

"Son, you have worked so hard for that hall lately," he pointed out. "Why don't you take a break and go out with your friends instead?" he suggested. Sam looked at his dad and said in a matter of fact tone. "It is my week to do whatever I want to do and I want to help get the hall ready for Stanley Horton's meetings."

Ben was proud of his partner and replied, "We always accept extra help."

Later that afternoon Ben and Sam approached the hall. To their surprise, other members shared the same thought. Almost twenty men were finishing cleaning the quarters with the scent of Pine-Sol ever present. A closer look showed the room was cleared of all dust with the floors shined. The tables even gave a reflection with the benches and chairs matching. They entered the hall and inspected the kitchen, bathrooms, and the enclosed area that sheltered those that had to live there. All was sterile as if it had just passed a military inspection.

"Hey, do you two have to do everything around here?" barked out the voice of Red Pennington. The father and son turned to see the old cuss cringing back at them with a duster in his hand. He was full of gusto and said, "We got this one covered. Why don't you guys go out and have a pizza?" he suggested.

They loved Red's spirit and looked at each other. "Dinner at Ella's?" asked the dad.

"That would be a fun!" answered the son. They left the building and Ben called his wife. "Honey," said Ben, "Sam and I are having a guy's night out tonight. We won't be home for dinner." Sam heard sound come from the receiver ending with his dad saying, "I love you too, bye." The Skates men walked to their favorite restaurant in town.

Upon entering the establishment, Ella herself greeted the dad and son. "Well," she said. "This is what we like to have around here." She knew where her favorite customers liked to sit and what pizza they usually ordered. She led them to the table where they sat down. Next she played the role of a psychic. Standing up straight she placed her right fingers on her forehead with her eyes closed. "I see a large pizza with sausage, peperoni, black olive, and extra cheese on thick crust." She muttered a sound foreign to the English language and continued to communicate. "And I see a picture of root beer with two glasses." Placing her hand alongside her body she finished, "The great Ella has spoken."

Ben and Sam cheered her performance and laughed. "You got it!" said Ben.

The soft drink came out first as Ella struck up a conversation. "What's this I hear about a new truck stop being built in town?" she asked. Ben looked at his son and motioned him to tell her about it. Sam started to talk to the entrepreneur. She pulled out a chair and sat in it backwards with her arms folded on the backrest.

When he was finished talking about Stanley Horton, Ella made a comment. "I wonder if it was that nice man that came in here this week. He was tan, wearing heavy prescription glasses, and asked me a few questions about this town." She touched her index finger on her chin as her memory became more focused. "In fact," she said, "I distinctly remember him mentioning your name, Ben, referring to you as a good friend."

Ben responded, "That was Stanley and we are good friends." Ella enjoyed hearing that.

"He was certainly a gentleman," she recalled. "He even left me a nice tip."

The guy's pizza night was long overdue and covered every humorous memory. It was now dark outside and the table was reduced to an empty pizza tray and vanished root beer. Ben felt proud having the money to afford this special moment. He rivaled Stanley Horton's tip and got up to put his jacket on. Together, they said goodbye to Ella and received a hug.

"Don't be a stranger," she said as they exited the front door.

"Not us," said Sam as he gave a thumbs up.

Ben and Sam were two doors away from their house as Mrs. Wilson noticeably waved from her living room window. They waved back and within moments were home sitting in front of the fireplace. All four family members were home on that winter night.

More good fortune entered the household. "Sam," called out the mother, "you got a letter in the mail today." She got up and went to the dining room table where she set it aside. She returned to the living room and handed it to him.

Sam looked at the envelope and jumped up with excitement. "Dad," he shouted out, "It's from State!"

The dad got up and stood next to his son. He saw the monogrammed envelope with the university's name and logo in the upper left hand corner. "Open it up," he said.

Sam opened the letter and found that he was offered a full-ride baseball scholarship. The son's trembling hand held the letter for his dad to read. Ben took the letter and scanned it. He immediately began to hug his boy while jumping up and down yelling, "You did it son, you did it!"

Chapter XIV

BEN SKATES WOKE UP feeling like the man he really was. His family was secure with each child one step closer to their dreams.

Today would be a special day; he was to meet with Stanley Horton for the inaugural nine o'clock meeting. There was also a special touch to the occasion; it was requested that his son attend as well if at all possible. That week's school schedule would allow Sam to join them.

Ben took a shower and dressed into a nice pressed outfit his wife had laid out for him. Sam was equally prepared with his favorite jeans and all-city jersey cleaned and pressed. It was a half hour before the meeting with the Skates men leaving for town. Ben and Sam soon entered the hall only to be greeted by Stanley Horton himself. "This place looks nice," he said. The professional was a stickler for detail and never overlooked an improvement of any measure. Ben was further impressed.

"Glad to see you again, Sam," said Stanley as he extended his hand.

Sam shook hands saying, "It's great to see you, Mr. Horton."

The teen was immediately corrected. "It's always *Stanley* to you," he said.

Sam looked at his dad with a grin and looked back at Stanley. "I like that, Stanley," he said.

"Well, good," he countered, "I like that too."

The corporate director became more personable as he raised his nose into the air and asked out loud. "Do you smell that?" The aroma of a warm, spicy, delicious breakfast waited for all who entered the hall. "Let's get in line and eat," he suggested.

They walked to the buffet and were overwhelmed with how long it was. Bacon, ham, scrambles eggs, and waffles awaited them as they made their way to the edge of the table to start the procession through the buffet.

At this moment, Ben looked around the room that normally served as a lounge for the fellowship members. He noticed a screen in front of the stage and drawing boards with illustrations on them. His fellowship members were properly dressed and mingling with newcomers who wore uniforms that matched the pens they were given. Their faces were of a clean, caring nature that expressed personality. All seemed interested in one another and above all, happy.

After their first pass through the buffet they sat down together and ate. The conversation with Stanley had nothing to do with business. It was just a neighborly visit that consisted of conversation that covered anything from fishing to childhood tales.

Soon, more got up to get seconds, with a few getting thirds, and one case a fourth trip. "This is good stuff," said Keven Worley, a former all-state wrestling champion.

Servers topped off coffee cups as the catering crew started to clear tables. One by one the chairs facing the stage began to fill. Stanley Horton was standing in front of the podium, signaling the start of the meeting.

The director for The Middle of the Road Oil Company was the consummate professional. He stood quiet to illustrate what he in turn needed before conducting the meeting. Once all were seated with everyone's undivided attention he spoke.

"On behalf of The Middle of the Road Oil Company, I am grateful to have all of you here." Stanley went to work displaying a map on the screen behind him. It clearly illustrated how desolate the location of the town was. He then showed how the new truck stop would be a haven for all motorists within hundreds of miles. From there, he explained how he was put on assignment to comb the far corners of the country to find where the middle of nowhere was.

His presentation slowly changed topics as he praised the character the town of Miner was made up of. He went into further detail explaining how the company's image matched the town's character. He began to share his experiences about randomly going through the community and about the people he met. He opened up about asking a select few questions to the locals, with all giving him the same answers. Eventually, he mentioned Ben Skates' name. "That's the name I've heard over and over again," said Stanley. "When I asked where a guy could go to get help they would answer with, 'Do you know who Ben Skates is?'

"The Middle of the Road Oil Company has many policies," Stanley pointed out. "One of which is to get the most respected home grown pillar of the community and appoint him or her to the highest position of a project. That person will have oversight over everything ranging from our training seminars to the actual construction site. From there, that person will be manager of our truck stop." With authority, Stanley had more information. "There is a former supply yard in this town that just closed its doors." That message struck a nerve with Ben; it was where he used to work.

"Our company just purchased that property and the acreage behind it," said Stanley Horton. "We wanted that land specifically to secure where someone has worked for many years. That person is who we want to dig the first shovel for this Saturday's groundbreaking ceremony that will happen at twelve noon. It will be somebody that this town believes in and that our company trusts."

Looking at Ben he boldly said, "That person is none other than Ben Skates." Stanley motioned for Ben to join him on stage as his wife, Gloria, came out from behind the curtains holding an extravagant bouquet of flowers with Susan following behind. Stanley pointed at Sam in the audience and said, "Get up here, Sam."

The entire Skates family was on stage receiving a standing ovation. Ben was definitely caught off guard as he kissed his wife and daughter and hugged his son. The man of the hour knew he had to say something, but he didn't know what. He walked next to Stanley and dwarfed him. Shaking hands, he said, "I promise to do my very best." Looking over the audience he commented, "Trust me, we have the guys to accomplish this task." He was finished with his speech with supportive friends cheering his name over and over again.

The meeting turned into a celebration for Ben. His family marveled as he walked off stage. They were happy for him as he was mobbed by pats, jabs, handshakes, and sincere compliments.

The week finished out and the month of March arrived, with Elmo still making his routine appearance at night. The climate slightly increased in temperature with the first day of rain taking place. Snow began to melt with warmer weather in the forecast. Training classes were held in the fellowship hall that week starting off with everyone being fitted for their company uniform.

The new outfits were something to be proud of. Attractive red sweaters with black and gray highlights were personalized. Each employee's name was monogrammed on the upper left side with the company logo underneath it. Black slacks with matching leather shoes completed the professional look.

Saturday came with Ben proudly taking hold of a shovel and scooping up the first shovel full of dirt as the township cheered the much advertised occasion. This was a major event for a small town with the local news on hand to interview Ben. Pictures were taken with his family, the mayor, and representatives from the oil company including Stanley Horton.

This was an important milestone. From that moment forward, the hall members were being paid by the day until the structure was complete, securing full-time jobs. Moral was high with everyone on the crew given a voucher to buy breakfast or lunch. The three month countdown was underway with the momentum in favor of the fellowship members.

Stanley Horton knew what he was doing when he picked Ben to lead. Around here he wasn't Mr. Skates, he was simply 'Ben'; the man everyone knew they could turn to.

As always, whether it was throughout the community, the fellowship hall, or the job site, he was a busy wearing every hat the job entailed. But the proud man wouldn't have it any other way.

Ben introduced himself to the contractors provided by the oil company. He coordinated who would help what professional as heavy equipment began to tear down the old aluminum warehouse where he once worked.

The job site was operating in a rhythm that surged the project forward. Ben stood back with pride as he watched every man work hard to make the deadline. He constantly roved the site to utilize his crew for maximum efficiency. Eventually, he walked to the fellowship hall to make his presence known. He watched a seminar that instructed on how to operate a cash register. He stayed there until he learned how to operate one. Then, he answered questions addressed to him from the class.

He returned to the job site in time to watch the construction crew complete their first day. Then he noticed a figure with a clipboard walking up to each worker. A closer look showed that it was Stanley Horton. He was paying each man a one hundred dollar bill and shaking their hand in appreciation for their hard work. Stanley noticed Ben and walked up to him. "There's one left and I know who earned it," he said. He handed Ben a bill and checked his name off the list. "That was a great performance today," complimented Stanley.

"Thank you," said Ben. "May I ask you a question?" he asked.

"Anything," said Stanley.

"Today is Saturday," Ben pointed out. "What days and hours do you want us to work?"

"All of that is up to you," he replied. "This is your show and you'll make those decisions. Just remember that I stuck my neck out there when I paid the bonus checks upfront."

"You have nothing to worry about," assured Ben. They shook hands wishing each other a good evening and parted. The local celebrity walked home to find his radiant flowers in a vase over the coffee table, its fragrance engulfing the entire room. Mrs. Wilson was sitting in front of the fireplace holding a cup of tea. "I saw you on the news today," she said with excitement.

Ben blushed saying, "You did, did you?"

Sharon was a lonely old lady that hungered for company and excitement. "Ben," she began to ask, "would you mind taking me to see this project sometime?"

Ben knew that she had an agenda to see where the new station was being built *now*. "Why, sure I can," he said. "In fact, I can show you where the new truck stop is being built right now."

Sharon's face lit up. She heard what she wanted to hear. The old woman quickly finished her tea, thanking Gloria. She immediately got up and walked to the door to get her coat. Sharon Wilson was going out that night!

Within minutes, they were in Ben's truck and slowly driving down Main Street. To the right was a lot of smooth dirt where they pulled into and parked. "This is what you saw on the news today," said Ben. Sharon Wilson looked from the truck and saw heavy equipment scattered about. There was also a portable white trailer with an enormous metal bin for scraps. Two mountains of twisted metal could be seen off to the side. She was bewildered to be surrounded by what appeared to be mass destruction. She was almost frightened and at a loss for words.

Ben was holding a picture of how graphic artists projected the truck stop to look like. He turned on the dome light and showed it to Sharon. She leaned towards the illustration to study it. Her eyes grew in size as her mouth opened with astonishment. Looking up she panned the surroundings in amazement that such an immaculate creation would soon be standing there.

Ben began to tell her what the truck stop would do. It was explained to her that it would always be open to serve anybody that needed fuel. But it will also cater to those that need to shop, get a warm meal, do laundry, or even stay the night. "We will not just have a restaurant, but also a coffee shop that serves sandwiches," he said.

The woman took a deep breath showing a confused look that only Edith Bunker could give. She concentrated while trying to fathom the complexity that was developing there. It then dawned on her that in her very own neighborhood, there would *always* be a place to go. She was relieved.

It started to sprinkle rain on the windshield. This was a blessing for Ben knowing that warmer weather would aid the outdoor project. He drove back home and escorted his neighbor to her front steps. "Thank you so much, Ben," she said giving a hug.

"You are quite welcome, Mrs. Wilson," he replied.

Ben went home and sat down at the dining room table with a pencil and paper. He jotted down how many workers he had and calculated how to split them up into two shifts. This would allow them to attend classes in the fellowship hall without slowing down the construction site. He also concentrated on what words to use when he would ask them to work twelve hour shifts, including Saturdays. Once his initial draft was made he called Troy Meeker to assist him.

It was late Saturday night with Ben and Troy having contacted the entire crew. Everything was understood and aligned with Ben's proposed work schedule. He would now take a shower and go to bed.

Sunday morning defiantly seemed like March. Steady rain had melted much of the snow leaving only the high piles left by snowplows and the glossy white fields in the distant foothills. Ben looked out his bedroom window and cheered on what nature was providing for him. He got into his bathrobe and went downstairs to meet his family for breakfast. Once seated at the table, he noticed the front page of the local newspaper resting before him. His picture shaking hands with the mayor graced the cover. He looked around and saw the loving eyes of his family staring back.

The Skates finished breakfast and picked up Sharon Wilson on their way to church. Later that day Ben chose to walk to town and access the job site. His goal was to search for any clues that would get the job further ahead. What he saw was a pleasant surprise.

Pete Rainwater, Emmitt Jenkins, Gene Fletcher, and at least ten others were unloading flatbed trucks that came the night before. The huge piles of scrap metal were already placed in the mammoth dumpster with the stage set for the contractors to immediately begin work. They were all just like Ben. Whatever sacrifice they could make for the cause, they would. Ben knew what to do. They were all grown men that always did *right*. He would leave without having to announce his arrival.

He turned around before he would be noticed and saw a figure standing by a secluded tree on an embankment. It was a medium sized man in a jean outfit wearing a denim hat. His arms were folded as he surveyed the progress through his dark prescription glasses.

Chapter XV

BEN WAS DRESSED AND ready to go to work. The conscientious foreman took the liberty the night before to load all of his tools in his truck. This would enable him to do as many extras as possible without having to wait for the contractors.

Monday morning had arrived. As Ben approached the front door fully dressed in his work clothes he noticed his lunchbox. It was placed on the stand next to the door with a message from Gloria taped on it. The message said how proud she was of him and on how much she loved him. He folded the letter, placed it in his pen pocket, and left the house.

He was almost in his truck when he heard a soft voice call out his name. He turned and saw Mrs. Wilson bundled up in warm clothes holding a plastic container of cookies. "Those men you are working with must be hungry," she said using her motherly skills. "Can you take me to them so that I can hand these out?" asked the woman imprisoned in loneliness.

It was Ben's practice to arrive early to work. He realized that he could take her down there to distribute cookies and still get her back home without being late. *Maybe this is what God wants* he thought to himself. "That would be a wonderful idea, Mrs.

Wilson," said Ben. "But we can't stay there long," he added. Ben took the cookies out of her hands and placed them in the cab. Next he helped her to the passenger seat and buckled her in.

Most of the crew was already present when Ben and Sharon Wilson arrived. He introduced Mrs. Wilson to them as she handed out her homemade chocolate chip cookies with walnuts. They were accepted and received great reviews after one bite. Sharon needed this and relished every second. The cookies disappeared fast with the men thanking her over and over again. "I'm sorry, Mrs. Wilson," said Ben in a warm tone. "We have to go back now."

The woman was satisfied having met more good men just like Ben. "It was nice meeting everyone," she said. "I'll go home and make some more."

"We'd love that, Mrs. Wilson," said Mike Talbot. Sharon's mission was accomplished with Ben driving her home and walking her to her front steps. "If there is anything I can do for them please let me know," she stressed.

"I will tell you immediately," he assured.

Ben returned to the site and watched the efficient flow of work get underway. The numbers were thinned out by those attending classes but no one wasted a step. He walked around the parameter and filled in where needed.

Sam Skates was also having an eventful day. He was flocked at school over his dad being featured in the local news. Sam had class and modestly down played the event. He also made the mistake of telling a mild-mannered science teacher about his scholarship offer. At lunch time, the news was all over school with Sam facing round two of compliments.

A poetic justice also surfaced, putting more icing on the cake. Ryan West did a poor job pretending to be happy for Sam. He had to break his congratulations into intervals as to not make his jealousy seem as obvious as it was. Every time he looked away, Sam could see the butterfly stitches on the side of his face from that rare ball that *mysteriously* got away from him. It was a permanent mark that forever enshrined a moment of the immature boy's life. Sam could hardly hold back the laughter as he pretended not to notice it.

Weeks passed with the new truck stop taking shape and Sam's high school years coming to a close. The rotation of classes intertwined with construction work kept ticking like a clock. On occasion, there would be a time-out to acknowledge care packages *personally* delivered from Sharon Wilson herself. Finally, the new truck stop was ready for business—two weeks before its deadline. This made Stanley Horton look good to the company. It also confirmed Ben Skates' reputation as a man, including those he shared a fellowship with. It was announced that there would be a meeting at The Men of Miner Fellowship Hall that evening at seven o'clock.

That night the hall was packed with everyone feeling a sense of accomplishment. Stanley walked up to the pulpit and said, "You did it guys!" He received the first round of applause as he continued. "There is one problem though," he said. "I was willing to pay you for three months work and I intend to." He held up a bag and pulled out an envelope that held one thousand dollars cash. He opened it up and displayed the ten one hundred dollar bills. "You earned this," he announced. He placed the money back into the envelope and dropped it into the bag. Next he called out to Ben and asked, "Can you hand these out for me?" Ben made his way to the stage and took the bag Stanley handed to him. He began to hand out the envelopes to the names printed on them as he checked them off a list.

Stanley asked for Ben to join him on stage. The big man got up there with Stanley as another round of applause circled the room. Stanley began to honor Ben's involvement with the project. Ben interrupted every time his name was mentioned by saying, "Us,"

"We," or "Everyone" audibility. It became a comedy skit with Stanley's wit harmlessly bouncing back as more and more laughter came from the room.

Stanley became more serious and talked about the ribbon cutting ceremony. He emphasized that 'one man should do us that honor.' Ben interrupted him by whispering into his ear. Stanley Horton froze as he listened. Stanley turned and whispered back to Ben and Ben whispered back again. Stanley nodded that he understood Ben's request and pointed at him saying, "Consider it done!"

It was obvious that Ben came through for the oil man and that he was indebted to him. Whatever Ben asked for was obviously granted. Something that they would not share with the hall that night and would have to wait until tomorrow.

Chapter XVI

IT WAS A CLEAR SATURDAY morning in May as Sharon Wilson fed her cat, Nightingale. The multicolored feline purred with its furry claws pulsating on the linoleum floor. It patiently looked up to her master as a bowl of canned food was placed on the mat next to her water dish. "You be good today until mother comes back," said the widow.

In recent years it seemed that the only ones in the lonely woman's life were her cat and the Skates family. In recent months that all seemed to change with the baked cookies and soup she made for the construction crew down the street. *She* was the old lady sitting in the front row at the wrestling shows.

Her telephone rang. She answered it and was pleased to hear that it was from the hero in her life: Ben Skates. "We'll be at your door in a few minutes," he said.

The woman was excited. She was invited to the ribbon cutting ceremony that would officially open up the new truck stop. The entire town would be there with the local news covering the event. The old woman was proud to be personally invited as a guest of Ben Skates.

She walked to the closet in the living room and got her coat, putting it on. Next she picked up her purse from the stand next to the door as someone knocked. The timing was perfect as she open the door.

She was greeted by a well-dressed Ben Skates wearing his company uniform. It was traditional for Ben to assure her safety and walk her to the sidewalk. "It's so nice to see you this morning, Ben," she said holding on to him. "Everyone is so proud of you."

"Well, everyone is proud of you too," he replied. Ben walked her to the sidewalk and acted as if he was waiting for something.

It turned out that he was.

A shiny semi painted red, black, and gray with The Middle of the Road Oil Company painted on its door approached them blasting its air horn. The woman stared at the beautiful truck and wondered what was going on. It passed by pulling a forty foot trailer with a matching paint scheme. In a minute it came back the opposite direction blasting its horn again and parking in front of Sharon and Ben.

Stanley Horton himself got out of the cab holding a light brown leather jacket with a matching western hat. "You make the best cookies in the whole world," he exclaimed as he approached Sharon. "And that soup of yours rivals my mother's."

The woman enjoyed the attention but was puzzled. "Do you know who I am?" he asked her.

"I'm not sure," she asked.

Stanley began to explain who he was and how he worked with Ben. "Our entire crew loves you," he said, "and we want you to have this as a gift from us." He held the front of the leather jacket towards her. It had her name written in pink on the upper left side with the company logo underneath it. Her mouth opened in shock.

"Let's take your coat off and put this on," suggested Ben. In a moment she was wearing her new jacket which fit perfectly.

"This will go just fine with it," said Stanley with assurance. He showed her the matching hat graced with a few feathers and placed it on her head.

Ben asked for her house keys to place her coat inside. They were handed to him and Ben went inside the home, returning empty handed.

"Mrs. Wilson," addressed Stanley with all his charm. "Will you please ride with me to the new truck stop we are about to open?"

The child came out in her as she looked at the semi. "I'd love that!" she exclaimed.

"Well, let's get you in there, girl," he said. Ben helped her get inside the luxurious eighteen wheeler and strapped her in. Closing the door, Stanley tooted the horn and drove down the street. Sharon was fascinated sitting up so high and riding in comfort. The world looked so different to her as the woman in the western hat peered over the dashboard with adventure in her eye.

He drove into the parking lot of the new truck stop tooting his horn, receiving cheers from hundreds. There were grand opening flags waving above the new station with beautiful floral displays suspended from planters that outlined the roof. To one side was rich green grass that had picnic tables, built in barbeques, and a community fire pit. To the opposite were many lanes that led to the many fuel pumps that were abreast. Behind that was a garage that could repair *anything*. Far behind it all was a laundry mat that advertised showers. Next to it was a modest two story motel that was painted gray and white and surrounded with plants.

Stanley drove up to the front doors blocked by a thick red ribbon. He parked and left the truck, walking around to assist Sharon. In a gentleman-type fashion he positioned his right arm to help her walk. The oil director led the woman up to the front door where Ben Skates was waiting. The media closed in on them as Stanley Horton greeted everyone. Microphones and cameras pushed their way to the front of the line as the festivities were about to begin.

"On behalf of The Middle of the Road Oil Company, I'd like to welcome everyone here," said the orator. Sharon Wilson was tense looking at the many faces looking back at her. Stanley began his speech. He talked about the town of Miner and the wholesome citizens it consisted of. He pointed out the values of the town and paralleled them with the standards his company stood for. Then he mentioned on how *it's the little people* that make the real difference. Stanley gave one local example after another to get his point across. Then he talked about the crew who built the structure that stood behind them and what they went through to beat a deadline.

Eventually, he commented about the wonderful homemade soup and the delicious cookies that were consistently prepared by Sharon Wilson. "A labor of love showed them that someone did care to keep their moral high," was how Stanley expressed it. He was telling the truth.

Sharon Wilson was shocked to hear her name mentioned. She'd *never* received credit like that in her whole life. Stanley then said, "We began this project with an unsung hero who has helped this community and we'll finish it with another one." The prestigious man looked to Sharon and handed her a large pair of scissors. She grabbed them as he asked, "Sharon, could you help these guys one more time by cutting the ribbon and opening up this station?"

Without thought, she followed her request and easily cut the ribbon in one attempt. From there cheers covered the entire neighborhood. Every man that worked on that project ran up and hugged the motherly image. Sam was in tears as he watched from the crowd. Gloria and Susan whistled with two fingers as if they were at a rodeo.

Once the frenzy died down, Stanley and Ben each pushed a glass door open, allowing Sharon Wilson to be the first person to enter the new building.

She took one step into the modern facility and stopped in her tracks. What she saw made her life stand still. Sharon was standing on shiny brown tile that branched off in different directions. The old woman started to tour the establishment. To her right was a coffee shop that had an enclosed area matching the company's colors. A closer look showed a counter where premiere deli sandwiches were served. Black wrought iron tables with matching chairs outlined the outside of the coffee shop, staying clear of foot traffic.

Ahead of her was a plush restaurant that matched the coffee shop. It had glass tables with etched glass used as partitions. Red curtains with black and gray carpet accented lavish paintings that hung on the walls. Floral displays covered every nook and cranny.

To her left was a grocery store that was joined by an automotive section. A crowd flowed into the new complex with employees taking their stations. Sharon walked by the store counters and continued outside. She had a clear view of the laundry mat which featured public restrooms that included showers. Sixty feet to the right of it was a quaint motel isolated within trees and ferns.

This truck stop is a vacation-land, she thought to herself. The celebrated woman re-entered the store in time to hear Ben loudly announce to his customers, "Attention everyone: today hotdogs, coffee, and pop are free."

Sharon Wilson was startled as a hand gently tapped her from behind. It was Stanley Horton saying, "C'mon girl, I'm buying you and the Skates' breakfast in the restaurant." Gloria put her arm around her saying, "Follow me."

The party of six were the first patrons to be served in the exotic diner. Once seated at their table, Sharon Wilson looked at the Skates family and Stanley Horton. She never felt so loved in her entire life. When the meal was finished, the group went back into the crowded station. In doing so, a tall, well-built African American man in a Stetson hat approached. His smile needed no introduction, it was Gene Fletcher.

The gracious man took off his hat and addressed her. "Those cookies and that soup you make are to die for," he said.

Sharon blushed and hugged the saintly man. "Now, I have a question to ask you," said Gene.

The woman gave her full attention as he spoke. "Are you aware of the beautiful flowers that cover Preston Valley this time of year?" he asked.

Her face grew in wonderment. "Preston Valley?" she questioned. "I've watched specials about it on television and seen pictures of it in magazines. I hear that it's beautiful there," she said in a quivery voice.

"Well," said Gene. "It just so happens that I have to deliver hay there today. I'd love to have your company on this trip." Gene was cute and pantomimed like a child by stretching out his arms saying, "It's only a half day trip there and back."

Sharon jumped on the chance and snapped, "I'd love to go!"

"Well, c'mon then," he answered. The big man put his hat back on and using his right arm, assisted her outside and into his semi. Once inside he asked his passenger, "Do you like Charlie Pride?"

The wild woman in the western hat said, "Everyone knows who Charlie is." Gene started to play Charlie Pride's Greatest Hits as they left the truck stop and motored down Main Street. Destination: Preston Valley.

The Middle of the Road Truck Stop would serve as a home away from home for Sharon Wilson. It was common for the night shift personnel to see her with a friend in the coffee shop. Some nights she could be seen in front of the fire pit sharing stories with the truckers. The lady never took the bus; drivers had adopted her and would pick her up in their rigs and later drive her back home. The Skates family was starting to miss her.

Sam and his friends put the truck stop on the top of their list for hangouts. One summer night, Ben was watching his son when a hungry trucker came in. He was obviously low on money. The stranger counted the change in his hand over and over again while staring at a large Italian grinder deli sandwich.

Sam approached him while pulling out a twenty dollar bill from his pant pocket. Ben watched his son give it to the starving trucker. The man *had* to accept it and expressively thanked him for it. Sam comforted the man by saying, "I'm glad I could help you." At that moment, the boy looked away and saw his dad looking back.

What happened next jolted a memory that took place in their home the past winter. It happened one night when Sharon Wilson was standing at their front door asking for help. Sam questioned his father's actions and confronted him later about it. A life lesson was taught ending with Sam repeating those immortal words shared that evening.

"After all," he said, "sometimes we all need a little help."

Ben looked at his son with an expression that read, "That's my boy." He nodded in approval and went back to his job.

That day was very special to Ben Skates. Earlier that evening he and his wife met Troy Meeker and his mother in the restaurant for dinner. Ben secretly handed Troy a roll of twenty dollar bills when they went to the restroom; money that Troy never kept track of or wanted back and a debt that Ben kept mental records of and *would* pay back.

It was a September evening in the Skates' household and Sam was dressed with his luggage resting by the front door. Soon, Ryan West would drive to their house in a car his father bought. From there the boys would leave for college.

Sam was already attacked by his mother, sister, and Mrs. Wilson. The college freshman was hugged and kissed many times over to the point where they were satisfied with their farewell. He was now left alone to share the last precious minutes with his father.

"I'm so proud of you," said the dad as he placed his right hand over Sam's shoulder and shook it.

"Thanks, dad," he replied. "I'm proud of you too."

"Son," said the dad, "last night I was cornered at the fellowship hall. The members wanted to vote in a new policy that lowers the age limit to join from twenty-one down to eighteen." He looked at his son and raised one eyebrow saying, "Apparently there is a young man in this town that will be turning eighteen in a few weeks and they want me to swear him in." The father raised his arms saying, "What could I do? They forced me to vote for that rule change."

Sam knew who his dad was referring to. *He* was about to turn eighteen. "I'd love to have you swear me in, dad," cried out the son as he hugged him. "You see, dad," he started to explain, "I will always love baseball but I want to go to college to get a degree. It's my turn to keep this town strong; just as you and grandpa have always done."

Ben paid close attention as a tear ran down his face. "I will play my very best baseball in college," he vowed. "But I am more interested in returning home as a Skates who coaches little league. That's more important to me than becoming a big-time major leaguer. I can get a degree in transportation, horticulture, even politics," he said. "Who knows, I might even be mayor of this town one day."

The father was impressed with the maturity level his son had developed. Pressing both hands on the sides of his face he stared into his eyes saying, "I will vote for you and you'll make a fine mayor for this town."

"I'll work *here* dad and we'll coach together," projected the son. The dad extended his arms and hugged his friend, his son.

Ryan pulled up in front of the house honking his horn. Sam let go of his dad, opened the door, and grabbed his luggage. "Bye, dad," he said, "and thanks for everything."

"Bye, son," he replied, "and good luck."

Sam charged out of the house, threw his luggage in the back seat, and left with Ryan.

Driving down Main Street Sam knew why Ryan wanted to drive him to college. He didn't get a scholarship and planned to walk on the team. The outfielder thought that by being associated with Sam, he would be placed at the same level; a theory that had already proven wrong in the past.

Sam pitied him because he knew that Ryan had already peaked as a baseball player. He also knew by looking at the driver's smug look that he was convinced he was destined for stardom. On occasion, Ryan would turn his head during small talk and expose the scar he would always carry – the one that marked the turning point of his career. They drove past the truck stop managed by Sam's dad and noticed the many semi-trucks lined up for fuel. There were also cars with people gathered at the fire pit.

Sam couldn't tell Ryan that he was losing interest in baseball as a livelihood. The town they were passing through was what he

---

wanted to be when he grew up. The students passed through the only traffic light in Miner and started to gain speed. Sam looked to the left and saw the fellowship hall that helped mentor him. He felt excitement knowing that soon he would be a lifetime member.

Ryan accelerated as he aimed the car towards the ramp that exited the small town. At that moment Sam felt a revelation. It was something that resembled a plague that was never recorded and had since vanished; something that only a man from The Men of Miner Fellowship Hall would understand. Going through Elm Street Sam looked to his right and saw a dream that had come true.

Elmo was gone.

Epilogue

The story of "Elmo" shows the continuation of the 'like father; like son' tradition this country was built on.

The town of Miner is a classic example. They were fortunate enough to have the Skates family every step of the way. Their accolades on the field reached out to newspapers far away giving recognition to the state's smallest town. That contribution was secondary however, for what they were known for off the field. They were great men who were also great baseball players. Men that pulled the weight of the entire town for three generations.

This story never left the region it took place in. It was important to show that the spirit and integrity within the community was all that was needed to prevail. All-American towns were created and sustained by such unity. Like Sam Skates, they also put forth a product that returns home one day, to carry on that tradition.

Author Biography

Matt Shea is a developing author having published five books. He is greatly inspired by the writings of Andy Griffith and focuses on the common folk that small towns are made of.

He credits the success of his first book, "The Groundskeeper And Other Short Stories" to his family. The values that were instilled throughout his childhood gave him the strong sense of justice that is conveyed through his writings. The Shea family is only an average American family from an average neighborhood. Their secret was that they were close knit and accepted others.

Matt's mother, Vyerl set an example of being self sacrificing; having never placed herself first. She always cared about the feelings of others, no matter who they were. She even sponsored many foster children despite having a family of eight. During the holidays, the Roman Catholic mom would also have a Hanukkah bush for their Jewish friends. There were years when the family would make Christmas gifts and personally deliver them to seniors in rest homes.

The very table that Matt writes all of his stories on came from a childhood neighbor, Netta Wilson. Through time, Netta had to be relocated to assistant living due to deteriorating health. Vyerl never forgot that she and Netta traveled to see the Vatican together. Care packages, visits, and transporting Netta to spend Sundays at their home became a ritual until her last day. When she passed away, Matt was bequeathed an antique table from Netta. A priceless heirloom that he regards as sacred.

Many of Matt's friends are senior citizens or foreign born. He has the common practice of brewing a pot of tea and inviting them over to watch Alfred Hitchcock. Together they will watch Alfred, share a cup of tea, and afterwords listen to his manuscripts. Sometimes these social gatherings last well beyond midnight. "This is where I get most of my ideas," says Matt. "I learned this from my mom."

Matt Shea appreciates all who take the time to read his stories. He loves feedback and offers his email address for any comments or suggestions you might have. Matt promises to do his very best to answer all who write him. His goal is to reach out to his audience and improve as a writer and a person.

worknmatt7@aol.com

Matt Shea and his daughter, Laura

www.ingramcontent.com/pod-product-compliance
Lightning Source LLC
Chambersburg PA
CBHW052140170626
46812CB00004B/1515